'IT'S A PROUD AND LONELY THING TO BE A STAINLESS STEEL RAT – AND IT'S THE GREATEST EXPERIENCE IN THE GALAXY IF YOU CAN GET AWAY WITH IT ...'

Society had more rats when the rules were looser, just as old wooden buildings had more rats than he concrete buildings that came later.

Now that society is all ferroconcrete and stainless steel, there are fewer gaps between the joints, and it takes a smart rat to find them. It takes a stainless steel rat – like Slippery Jim diGriz.

When the legendary Special Corps finally corner Slippery Jim, they have two choices: Either kill him (no easy task) – or hire the notorious criminal for one-way assignments to the weirdest and deadliest planets in the galaxy.

The choice is simple.

The interstellar outlaw is about to become one hell of an interstellar cop ...

Harry Harrison is the author of numerous science fiction and fantasy novels. He was described by Philip K. Dick as 'the iconoclast of the known universe' and by the *Daily Telegraph* as 'the Monty Python of the spaceways'. His Stainless Steel Rat books made their debut in the early 'sixties and have been one of SF's most popular series ever since. Harry Harrison lives in Ireland.

Also available from Orion/Millennium

The Stainless Steel Rat's Revenge
The Stainless Steel Rat Goes to Hell

—THE—
STAINLESS
STEEL RAT

Harry Harrison

MILLENNIUM

Orion Paperbacks
A Millennium Book
First published in Great Britain in 1966
This paperback edition published in 1997
by Orion Books Ltd,
Orion House, 5 Upper St Martin's Lane, London, WC2H 9EA

A CIP catalogue record for this book is available
from the British Library.

ISBN: 1 85798 498 6

Typeset by Deltatype Limited, Birkenhead, Merseyside
Printed and bound in Great Britain by
Clays Ltd, St Ives plc

A DEVILISH GOOD
PIECE OF ADVICE

Jim diGriz has a swollen ego these days, ever since he discovered that his annals have been published in a great number of countries and languages. In addition to the American and English editions his adventures have been read in all of the Western European countries, as well as in Japan and China. Since glasnost he has penetrated Russia, Poland, and Estonia. A total of fifteen countries. And very soon now we will see the first publication of *Rustimuna Ŝtalrato Naskiĝas*. That's *The Rat Is Born* in Esperanto.

Esperanto? There's that word again. We know that Jim speaks it like a native. As does almost everyone else he meets. But does it exist in the present?

It certainly does. It is a growing, living language with millions of speakers right around the world. It is easy to learn and fun to use – and a lot more practical than Klingon. There are many books, magazines, and even newspapers published in Esperanto.

So be the first on your street to enjoy the excitement and fun. Put your name and address on a postcard and send it to this address:

Esperanto
PO Box 1129
El Cerrito, CA 94530
USA

Tell them the Rat sent you. You will never regret it!

– *Harry Harrison*

CHAPTER

— 1 —

When the office door opened suddenly I knew the game was up. It had been a money-maker – but it was all over. As the cop walked in I sat back in the chair and put on a happy grin. He had the same somber expression and heavy foot that they all have – and the same lack of humor. I almost knew to the word what he was going to say before he uttered a syllable.

'James Bolivar diGriz I arrest you on the charge—'

I was waiting for the word *charge*, I thought it made a nice touch that way. As he said it I pressed the button that set off the charge of black powder in the ceiling, the crossbeam buckled and the three-ton safe dropped through right on the top of the cop's head. He squashed very nicely, thank you. The cloud of plaster dust settled and all I could see of him was one hand, slightly crumpled. It twitched a bit and the index finger pointed at me accusingly. His voice was a little muffled by the safe and sounded a bit annoyed. In fact he repeated himself a bit.

'... On the charge of illegal entry, theft, forgery—'

He ran on like that for quite a while, it was an impressive list but I had heard it all before. I didn't let it interfere with my stuffing all the money from the desk drawers into my suitcase. The list ended with a new charge and I would swear on a stack of thousand credit notes *that* high that there was a hurt tone in his voice.

'In addition the charge of assaulting a police robot will be added to your record. This was foolish since my brain and larynx are armored and in my midsection—'

'That I know well, George, but your little two-way radio is in the top of your pointed head and I don't want you reporting to your friends just yet.'

One good kick knocked the escape panel out of the wall and gave access to the steps to the basement. As I skirted the rubble on the floor the robot's fingers snapped out at my leg, but I had been waiting for that and they closed about two inches short. I have been followed by enough police robots to know by now how indestructible they are. You can blow them up or knock them down and they keep coming after you; dragging themselves by one good finger and spouting saccharine morality all the while. That's what this one was doing. Give up my life of crime and pay my debt to society and such. I could still hear his voice echoing down the stairwell as I reached the basement.

Every second was timed now. I had about three minutes before they would be on my tail, and it would take me exactly one minute and eight seconds to get clear of the building. That wasn't much of a lead and I would need all of it. Another kick panel opened out into the label-removing room. None of the robots looked up as I moved down the aisle – I would have been surprised if they had. They were all low-grade M types, short on brains and good only for simple, repetitive work. That was why I hired them. They had no curiosity as to why they were taking the labels off

2

the filled cans of azote fruits, or what was at the other end of the moving belt that brought the cans through the wall. They didn't even look up when I unlocked the Door That Was Never Unlocked that led through the wall. I left it open behind me as I had no more secrets now.

Keeping next to the rumbling belt, I stepped through the jagged hole I had chopped in the wall of the government warehouse. I had installed the belt too, this and the hole were the illegal acts that I had to do myself. Another locked door opened into the warehouse. The automatic fork-lift truck was busily piling cans onto the belt and digging fresh ones out of the ceiling-high piles. This fork-lift had hardly enough brains to be called a robot, it just followed taped directions to load the cans. I stepped around it and dog-trotted down the aisle. Behind me the sounds of my illegal activity died away. It gave me a warm feeling to still hear it going full blast like that.

It *had* been one of the nicest little rackets I had ever managed. For a small capital outlay I had rented the warehouse that backed on the government warehouse. A simple hole in the wall and I had access to the entire stock of stored goods, long-term supplies that I knew would be untouched for months or years in a warehouse this size. Untouched, that is, until I came along.

Afer the hole had been made and the belt installed it was just a matter of business. I hired the robots to remove the old labels and substitute the colorful ones I had printed. Then I marketed my goods in a strictly legal fashion. My stock was the best and due to my imaginative operation my costs were very low. I could afford to undersell my competitors and still make a handsome profit. The local wholesalers had been quick to sense a bargain and I had orders for months ahead. It *had* been a good operation – and could have gone on for quite a while.

I stifled that train of thought before it started. One lesson that has to be remembered in my line of business is that when an operation is over it is OVER! The temptation to stay just one more day or to cash just one more check can be almost overwhelming, ah, how well I know. I also know that it is also the best way to get better acquainted with the police.

Turn your back and walk away—
And live to graft another day.

That's my motto and it's a good one. I got where I am because I stuck to it.

And daydreams aren't part of getting away from the police.

I pushed all thoughts from my mind as I reached the end of the aisle. The entire area outside must have been swarming with cops by this time and I had to move fast and make no mistakes. A fast look right and left. Nobody in sight. Two steps ahead and press the elevator button. I had put a meter on this back elevator and it showed that the thing was used once a month on the average.

It arrived in about three seconds, empty, and I jumped in, thumbing the roof button at the same time. The ride seemed to go on forever, but that was just subjective. By the record it was exactly fourteen seconds. This was the most dangerous part of the trip. I tightened up as the elevator slowed. My .75 caliber

4

recoilless was in my hand, that would take care of one cop, but no more.

The door shuffled open and I relaxed. Nothing. They must have the entire area covered on the ground so they hadn't bothered to put cops on the roof.

In the open air now I could hear the sirens for the first time – a wonderful sound. They must have had half of entire police force out from the amount of noise they were making. I accepted it as any artist accepts tribute.

The board was behind the elevator shaft where I had left it. A little weather-stained but still strong. A few seconds to carry it to the edge of the parapet and reach it across to the next building.

Gently, this was the one dangerous spot where speed didn't count. Carefully onto the end of the board, the suitcase held against my chest to keep my center of gravity over the board. One step at a time. A thousand-foot drop to the ground. If you don't look down you can't fall ...

Over. Time for speed. The board behind the parapet, if they didn't see it at first my trail would be covered for a while at least. Ten fast steps and there was the door to the stairwell. It opened easily – and it better have – I had put enough oil on the hinges. Once inside I threw the bolt and took a long, deep breath. I wasn't out of it yet, but the worst part where I ran the most risk was past. Two uninterrupted minutes here and they would never find James Bolivar, alias 'Slippery Jim', diGriz.

The stairwell at the roof was a musty, badly lit cubicle that was never visited. I had checked it carefully a week before for phono and optic bugs and it had been clear. The dust looked undisturbed, except for my own footprints. I had to take a chance that it hadn't been bugged since then. The calculated risk must be accepted in this business.

Good-by James diGriz, weight ninety-eight kilos, age about forty-five, thick in the middle and heavy in the jowls, a typical business man whose picture graces the police files of a thousand planets – also his fingerprints. They went first. When you wear them they feel like a second skin, a touch of solvent though and they peel off like a pair of transparent gloves.

All my clothes next – and then the girdle in reverse – that lovely paunch that straps around my belly and holds twenty kilos of lead mixed with thermite. A quick wipe from the bottle of bleach and my hair was its natural shade of brown, the eyebrows, too. The nose plugs and cheek pads hurt coming out, but that only lasts a second. Then the blue-eyed contact lenses. This process leaves me mother-naked and I always feel as if I have been born again. In a sense it is true, I had become a new man, twenty kilos lighter, ten years younger and with a completely different description. The large suitcase held a complete change of clothes and a pair of dark-rimmed glasses that replaced the contact lenses. All the loose money fitted neatly into a brief case.

When I straightened up I really felt as if ten years had been stripped from me. I was so used to wearing that weight that I never noticed it – until it was gone. Put a real spring in my step.

The thermite would take care of all the evidence. I kicked it all into a heap and triggered the fuse. It caught with a roar and bottles, clothes, bag, shoes, weights, et al, burned with a cheerful glare. The police would find a charred spot on the cement and microanalysis might get them a few molecules off the walls, but that was all they would get. The glare of the burning thermite threw jumping shadows around me as I walked down three flights to the one hundred twelfth floor.

Luck was still with me, there was no one on the floor when I opened the door. One minute later the express elevator let me and a handful of other business types out into the lobby.

Only one door was open to the street and a portable TV camera was trained on it. No attempt was being made to stop people from going in and out of the building, most of them didn't even notice the camera and little group of cops around it. I walked towards it at an even pace. Strong nerves count for a lot in this business.

For one instant I was square in the field of that cold, glass eye, then I was past. Nothing happened so I knew I was clear. That camera must have fed directly to the main computer at police headquarters. If my description had been close enough to the one they had on file those robots would have been notified and I would have been pinned before I had taken a step. You can't outmove a computer-robot combination, not when they move and react in microseconds – but you can outthink them. I had done it again.

A cab took me about ten blocks away. I waited until it was out of sight then took another one. It wasn't until I was in the third cab that I felt safe enough to go to the space terminal. The sounds of sirens were growing fainter and fainter behind me and only an occasional police car tore by in the opposite direction. They were sure making a big fuss over a little larceny but that's the way it goes on these overcivilized worlds. Crime is such a rarity now that the police really get carried away when they run across some. In a way I can't blame them, giving out traffic tickets must be an awful dull job. I really believe they ought to thank me for putting a little excitement in their otherwise dull lives.

CHAPTER

— 2 —

It was a nice ride to the spaceport being located, of course, far out of town. I had time to lean back and watch the scenery and gather my thoughts. Even time to be a little philosophical. For one thing I could enjoy a good cigar again, I smoked only cigarettes in my other personality and never violated that personality, even in strictest privacy. The cigars were still fresh in the pocket humidor where I had put them six months ago. I sucked a long mouthful and blew the smoke out at the flashing scenery. It was good to be off the job, just about as good as being on it. I could never make my mind up which period I enjoyed more – I guess they are both right at the time.

My life is so different from that of the overwhelming majority of people in our society that I doubt if I could even explain it to them. They exist in a fat, rich union of worlds that have almost forgotten the meaning of the word crime. There are few malcontents and even fewer that are socially maladjusted. The few of these that are born, in spite of centuries of genetic control, are caught early and the aberration quickly adjusted. Some don't show their weakness until they are adults, they are the ones who try their hand at petty crime –

burglary, shoplifting or such. They get away with it for a week or two or a month or two, depending on the degree of their native intelligence. But sure as atomic decay – and just as predestined – the police reach out and pull them in.

That is almost the full extent of crime in our organized, dandified society. Ninety-nine per cent of it, let's say. It is that last and vital one per cent that keeps the police departments in business. That one per cent is me, and a handful of men scattered around the galaxy. Theoretically we can't exist, and if we do exist we can't operate – but we do. We are the rats in the wainscoting of society – we operate outside of their barriers and outside of their rules. Society had more rats when the rules were looser, just as the old wooden buildings had more rats than the concrete buildings that came later. But they still had rats. Now that society is all ferroconcrete and stainless steel there are fewer gaps between the joints, and it takes a smart rat to find them. A stainless steel rat is right at home in this environment.

It is a proud and lonely thing to be a stainless steel rat – and it is the greatest experience in the galaxy if you can get away with it. The sociological experts can't seem to agree why we exist, some even doubt that we do. The most widely accepted theory says that we are victims of delayed psychological disturbance that shows no evidence in childhood when it can be detected and corrected and only appears later in life. I have naturally given a lot of thought to the topic and I don't hold with that idea at all.

A few years back I wrote a small book on the subject – under a nom de plume of course – that was rather well received. My theory is that the aberration is a philosophical one, not a psychological one. At a certain stage the realization strikes through that one must either live outside of society's bonds or die of absolute boredom. There is no future or freedom in the circumscribed life and the only other life is complete rejection of the rules. There is no longer room for the soldier of fortune or the gentleman adventurer who can live both within and ouside of society. Today it is all or nothing. To save my own sanity I chose the nothing.

The cab just reached the spaceport as I hit on this negative line of thought and I was glad to abandon it. Loneliness is the thing to fear in this business, that and self-pity can destroy you if they get the upper hand. Action has always helped me, the elation of danger and escape always clears my mind. When I paid the cab I shortchanged the driver right under his nose, palming one of the credit notes in the act of handing it to him. He was blind as a riveted bulkhead, his gullibility had me humming with delight. The tip I gave him more than made up the loss since I only do this sort of petty business to break the monotony.

There was a robot clerk behind the ticket window, he had that extra third eye in the center of his forehead that meant a camera. It clicked slightly as I purchased a ticket, recording my face and destination. A normal precaution on the part of the police, I would have been surprised if it hadn't happened. My destination was inter-system so I doubted if the picture would appear any place except the files. I wasn't making an interstellar hop this time, as I usually did after a big job, it wasn't necessary. After a job a single world or a small system is too small for more work, but Beta Cygnus has a system of almost twenty planets all with terrafied weather. This planet, III, was too hot now, but the rest of the system was wide open. There was a lot of commercial rivalry within the system and I knew their police departments didn't co-operate too well. They would pay the price for that. My ticket was for Moriy, number XVIII, a large and mostly agricultural planet.

There were a number of little stores at the space-sport. I shopped them carefully and outfitted a new suitcase with a complete wardrobe and traveling essentials. The tailor was saved for last. He ran up a couple of traveling suits and a formal kilt for me and I took them into the fitting booth. Strictly by accident I managed to hang one of the suits over the optic bug in the wall and made undressing sounds with my feet while I doctored the ticket I had just bought. The other end of my cigar cutter was a punch; with it I altered the keyed holes that indicated my destination. I was now going to planet X, not XVIII, and I had lost almost two hundred credits with the alteration. That's the secret of ticket and order changing. Don't raise the face value – there is too good a chance that this will be noticed. If you lower the value and lose money on the deal, even if it is caught, people will be sure it is a mistake on the machine's part. There is never the shadow of a doubt, since why should anyone change a ticket to lose money?

Before the police could be suspicious I had the suit off the bug and tried it on, taking my time. Almost everything was ready now, I had about an hour to kill before the ship left. I spent the time wisely by going to an automatic cleaner and having all my new clothes cleaned and pressed. Nothing interests a customs man more than a suitcase full of unworn clothes.

Customs was a snap and when the ship was about half full I boarded her and took a seat near the hostess. I flirted with her until she walked away, having classified me in the category of MALE, BRASH, ANNOYING. An old girl who had the seat next to mine also had me filed in the same drawer and was looking out of the window with obvious ice on her shoulder. I dozed off happily since there is one thing better than not being noticed and that is being noticed and filed into a category. Your description gets mixed up with every other guy in the file and that is the end of it.

When I woke up we were almost to planet X, I half dozed in the chair until we touched down, then smoked a cigar while my bag cleared customs. My locked brief case of money raised no suspicions since I had foresightedly forged papers six months ago with my occupation listed as *bank messenger*. Interplanet credit was almost nonexistent in this system, so the customs men were used to seeing a lot of cash go back and forth.

Almost by habit I confused the trail a little more and ended up in the large manufacturing city of Brouggh over one thousand kilometers from the point where I had landed. Using an entirely new set of identification papers I registered at a quiet hotel in the suburbs.

Usually after a big job like this I rest up for a month or two; this was one time though I didn't feel like a rest. While I was making small purchases around town to rebuild the personality of James diGriz, I was also keeping my eyes open for new business opportunities. The very first day I was out I saw what looked like a natural – and each day it looked better and better.

One of the main reasons I have stayed out of the

arms of the law for as long as I have, is that I have never repeated myself. I have dreamed up some of the sweetest little rackets, run them off once, then stayed away from them forever after. About the only thing they had in common was the fact that they all made money. About the only thing I hadn't hit to date was out and out armed robbery. It was time for a change and it looked like that was it.

While I was rebuilding the paunchy personality of Slippery Jim I was making plans for the operation. Just about the time the fingerprint gloves were ready the entire business was planned. It was simple like all good operations should be, the less details there are, the less things there are that can go wrong.

I was going to hold up Moraio's, the largest retail store in the city. Every evening at exactly the same time, an armored car took the day's receipts to the bank. It was a tempting prize – a gigantic sum in untraceable small bills. The only real problem as far as I was concerned was how one man could handle the sheer bulk and weight of all that money. When I had an answer to that the entire operation was ready.

All the preparations were, of course, made only in my mind until the personality of James diGriz was again ready. The day I slipped that weighted belly back on, I felt I was back in uniform. I lit my first cigarette almost with satisfaction, then went to work. A day or two for some purchases and a few simple thefts and I was ready. I scheduled the following afternoon for the job.

A large tractor-truck that I had bought was the key to the operation – along with some necessary alterations I had made to the interior. I parked the truck in an 'L' shaped alley about a half mile from Moraio's.

The truck almost completely blocked the alley but that wasn't important since it was used only in the early morning. It was a leisurely stroll back to the department store, I reached it at almost the same moment that the armored truck pulled up. I leaned against the wall of the gigantic building while the guards carried out the money. My money.

To someone of little imagination I suppose it would have been an awe-inspiring sight. At least five armed guards standing around the entrance, two more inside the truck as well as the driver and his assistant. As an added precaution there were three monocycles purring next to the curb. They would go with the truck as protection on the road. Oh, very impressive. I had to stifle a grin behind my cigarette when I thought about what was going to happen to those elaborate precautions.

I had been counting the handtrucks of money as they rolled out of the door. There were always fifteen, no more, no less; this practice made it easy for me to know the exact time to begin. Just as fourteen was being loaded into the armored truck, load number fifteen appeared in the store entrance. The truck driver had been counting the way I had, he stepped down from the cab and moved to the door in the rear in order to lock it when loading was finished.

We synchronized perfectly as we strolled by each other. At the moment he reached the rear door I reached the cab. Quietly and smoothly I climbed up into it and slammed the door behind me. The assistant had just enough time to open his mouth and pop his eyes when I placed an anesthetic bomb on his lap; he slumped in an instant. I was, of course, wearing the correct filter plugs in my nostrils. As I started the motor with my left hand, I threw a larger bomb through the connecting window to the rear with my right. There were some reassuring thumps as the guards there dropped over the bags of change.

This entire process hadn't taken six seconds. The guards on the steps were just waking up to the fact that something was wrong. I gave them a cheerful wave through the window and gunned the armored truck away from the curb. One of them tried to run and throw himself through the open rear door but he was a little too late. It all had happened so fast that not one of them had thought to shoot, I had been sure there would be a *few* bullets. The sedentary life on these planets does slow the reflexes.

The monocycle drivers caught on a lot faster, they were after me before the truck had gone a hundred feet. I slowed down until they had caught up, then stamped on the accelerator, keeping just enough speed so they couldn't pass me.

Their sirens were screaming, of course, and they had their guns working; it was just as I had planned. We tore down the street like jet racers and the traffic melted away before us. They didn't have time to think and realize that *they* were making sure the road was clear for my escape. The situation was very humorous and I'm afraid I chuckled out loud as I tooled the truck around the tight corners.

Of course the alarm had been turned in and the road blocks must have been forming up ahead – but that half mile went by fast at the speed we were doing. It was a matter of seconds before I saw the alley mouth ahead. I turned the truck into it, at the same time pressing the button on my pocket short wave.

Along the entire length of the alley my smoke bombs ignited. They were, of course, home made, as was all my equipment, nevertheless they produced an adequately dense cloud in that narrow alley. I pulled the truck a bit to the right until the fenders scraped the wall and only slightly reduced my speed, this way I could steer by touch. The monocycle drivers, of course, couldn't do this and had the choice of stopping or rushing headlong into the darkness. I hope they made the right decision and none of them were hurt.

The same radio impulse that triggered the bombs was supposed to have opened the rear door of the trailer truck up ahead and dropped the ramp. It had worked fine when I had tested it, I could only hope now that it did the same in practice. I tried to estimate the distance I had gone in the alley by timing my speed, but I was a little off. The front wheels of the truck hit the ramp with a destructive crash and the armored truck bounced rather than rolled into the interior of the larger van. I was jarred around a bit and had just enough sense left to jam on the brakes before I plowed right through into the cab.

Smoke from the bombs made a black midnight of everything, that and my shaken-up brains almost ruined the entire operation. Valuable seconds went by while I leaned against the truck wall trying to get oriented. I don't know how long it took, when I finally did stumble back to the rear door I could hear the guards' voices calling back and forth through the smoke. They heard the bent ramp creak as I lifted it so I threw two gas bombs out to quiet them down.

The smoke was starting to thin as I climbed up to the cab of the tractor and gunned it into life. A few feet down the alley and I broke through into sunlight. The alley mouth opened out into a main street a few feet ahead and I saw two police cars tear by. When the truck reached the street I stopped and took careful note of all witnesses. None of them showed any interest in the truck or the alley. Apparently all the commotion was still at the other end of the alley. I poured power into the engine and rolled out into the street, away from the store I had just robbed.

Of course I only went a few blocks in that direction, then turned down a side street. At the next corner I turned again and headed back towards Moraio's, the scene of my recent crime. The cool air coming in the window soon had me feeling better, I actually whistled a bit as I threaded the big truck through the service roads.

It would have been fine to go up the highway in front of Moraio's and see all the excitement, but that would have been only asking for trouble. Time was still important. I had carefully laid out a route that avoided all congested traffic and this was what I followed. It was only a matter of minutes before I was pulling into the loading area in the back of the big store. There was a certain amount of excitement here but it was lost in the normal bustle of commerce. Here and there a knot of truck drivers or shipping foremen were exchanging views on the robbery, since robots don't gossip the normal work was going on. The men were, of course, so excited that no attention was paid to my truck when I pulled into the parking line next to the other vans. I killed the engine and settled back with a satisfied sigh.

The first part was complete. The second part of the operation was just as important though. I dug into my paunch for the kit that I always take on the job – for just such an emergency as this. Normally, I don't believe in stimulants, but I was still groggy from the banging around. Two cc's of Linoten in my ante cubital cleared that up quickly enough. The spring was back in my step when I went into the back of the van.

The driver's assistant and the guards were still out and would stay that way for at least ten hours. I arranged them in a neat row in the front of the truck where they wouldn't be in my way, and went to work.

The armored car almost filled the body of the trailer as I knew it would; therefore I had fastened the boxes to the walls. They were fine, strong shipping boxes with Moraio's printed all over them. It had been a minor theft from their warehouse that should go unnoticed. I pulled the boxes down and folded them for packing, I was soon sweating and had to take my shirt off as I packed the money bundles into the boxes.

It took almost two hours to stuff and seal the boxes with tape. Every ten minutes or so I would check through the peephole in the door; only the normal activities were going on. The police undoubtedly had the entire town sealed and were tearing it apart building by building looking for the truck. I was fairly sure that the last place they would think of looking was the rear of the robbed store.

The warehouse that had provided the boxes had also provided a supply of shipping forms. I fixed one of these on each box, addressed to different pick-up addresses and marked paid, of course, and was ready to finish the operation.

It was almost dark by this time; however I knew that the shipping department would be busy most of the night. The engine caught on the first revolution and I pulled out of the parking rank and backed slowly up to the platform. There was a relatively quiet area where the shipping dock met the receiving dock, I stopped the trailer as close to the dividing line as I could. I didn't open the rear door until all the workmen were faced in a different direction. Even the stupidest of them would have been interested in why a truck was unloading the firm's own boxes. As I piled them up on the platform I threw a tarp over them, it only took a few minutes. Only when the truck gates were closed and locked did I pull off the tarp and sit down on the boxes for a smoke.

It wasn't a long wait. Before the cigarette was finished a robot from the shipping department passed close enough for me to call him.

'Over there. The M-19 that was loading these burned out a brakeband, you better see that they're taken care of.'

His eyes glowed with the light of duty. Some of these higher M types take their job very seriously. I had to step back quickly as the fork lifts and M-trucks appeared out of the doors behind me. There was a scurry of loading and sorting and my haul vanished down the platform. I lighted another cigarette and watched for a while as the boxes were coded and stamped and loaded on the outgoing trucks and local belts.

All that was left for me now was the disposing of the truck on some side street and changing personalities.

As I was getting into the truck I realized for the first time that something was wrong. I, of course, had been keeping an eye on the gate – but not watching it closely enough. Trucks had been going in and out. Now the realization hit me like a hammer blow over the solar plexus. They were the same trucks going both ways. A large, red cross-country job was just pulling out. I heard the echo of its exhaust roar down the street – then die away to an idling grumble. When it roared up again it didn't go away, instead the truck came in through the second gate. There were police cars waiting outside that wall. Waiting for me.

CHAPTER

—3—

For the first time in my career I felt the sharp fear of the hunted man. This was the first time I had ever had the police on my trail when I wasn't expecting them. The money was lost, that much was certain, but I was no longer concerned with that. It was me they were after now.

Think first, then act. I was safe enough for the moment. They were, of course, moving in on me, going slowly as they had no idea of where I was in the giant loading yard. How had they found me? *That* was the important point. The local police are used to an almost crimeless world, they couldn't have found my trail this quickly. In fact, I hadn't left a trail. Whoever had set the trap here had done it with logic and reason.

Unbidden the words jumped into my mind.

The Special Corps.

Nothing was ever printed about it, only a thousand whispered words heard on a thousand worlds around the galaxy. The Special Corps, the branch of the League that took care of the troubles that individual planets couldn't solve. The Corps was supposed to have finished off the remnants of Haskell's Raiders after the peace, of putting the illegal T & Z Traders out of business, of finally catching Inskipp. And now they were after me.

They were out there waiting for me to make a break. They were thinking of all the ways out just as I was — and they were blocking them. I had to think fast and I had to think right.

Only two ways out. Through the gates or through the store. The gates were too well covered to make a break, in the store there would be other exits. It had to be that way. Even as I made the conclusion I knew that other minds had made it too, that men were moving in to cover those doors. That thought brought fear — and made me angry as well. The very idea that someone could outthink me was odious. They could try all right — but I would give them a run for their money. I still had a few tricks left.

First, a little misdirection. I started the truck, left it in low gear and aimed it at the gate. When it was going straight I locked the steering wheel with the friction clamp and dropped out the far side of the cab and strolled back to the warehouse. Once inside I moved faster. Behind me I heard some shots, a heavy crump, and a lot of shouting. That was more like it.

The night locks were connected on the doors that led to the store proper. An old-fashioned alarm that I could disconnect in a few moments. My pick-locks opened the door and I gave it a quick kick with my foot and turned away. There were no alarm bells, but I knew that somewhere in the building an indicator showed that the door was opened. As fast as I could run I went to the last door on the opposite side of the building. This time I made sure the alarm was disconnected before I went through the door. I locked it behind me.

It is the hardest job in the world to run and be quiet at the same time. My lungs were burning before I reached the employees' entrance. A few times I saw flashing lights ahead and had to double down different aisles, it was mostly luck that I made it without being spotted. There were two men in uniform standing in front of the door I wanted to go out of. Keeping as close to the wall as I could, I made it to within twenty feet of them before I threw the gas grenade. For one second I was sure that they had gas masks on and I had reached the end of the road – then they slumped down. One of them was blocking the door, I rolled him aside and slid it open a few inches.

The searchlight couldn't have been more than thirty feet from the door; when it flashed on the light was more pain than glare. I dropped the instant it came on and the slugs from the machine pistol ate a line of glaring holes across the door. My ears were numb from the roar of the exploding slugs and I could just make out the thud of running footsteps. My own .75 was in my hand and I put an entire clip of slugs through the door, aiming high so I wouldn't hurt anyone. It would not stop them, but it should slow them down.

They returned the fire, must have been a whole squad out there. Pieces of plastic flew out of the back wall and slugs screamed down the corridor. It was good cover, I knew there was nobody coming up behind me. Keeping as flat as I could I crawled in the opposite direction, out of the line of fire. I turned two corners before I was far enough from the guns to risk standing up. My knees were shaky and great blobs of color kept fogging my vision. The searchlight had done a good job, I could barely see at all in the dim light.

I kept moving slowly, trying to get as far away from the gunfire as possible. The squad outside had fired as soon as I opened the door, that meant standing orders to shoot at anyone who tried to leave the building. A nice trap. The cops inside would keep looking until they found me. If I tried to leave I would be blasted. I was beginning to feel very much like a trapped rat.

Every light in the store came on and I stopped, frozen. I was near the wall of a large farm-goods showroom. Across the room from me were three soldiers. We spotted each other at the same time, I dived for the door with bullets slapping all around me. The military was in it too, they sure must have wanted me bad. A bank of elevators was on the other side of the door – and stairs leading up. I hit the elevator in one bounce and punched the sub-basement button, and just got out ahead of the closing doors. The stairs were back towards the approaching soldiers, I felt like I was running right into their guns. I must have made the turn into the stairs a split second ahead of their arrival. Up the stairs and around the first landing before they were even with the bottom. Luck was still on my side. They hadn't seen me and were sure I had gone down. I sagged against the wall, listening to the shouts and whistle blowing as they turned the hunt towards the basement.

There was one smart one in the bunch. While the others were all following the phony trail I heard him start slowly up the stairs. I didn't have any gas grenades left, all I could do was climb up ahead of him, trying to do it without making a sound.

He came on slowly and steadily and I stayed ahead

of him. We went up four flights that way, me in my stockinged feet with my shoes around my neck, his heavy boots behind me making a dull rasping on the metal stairs.

As I started up the fifth flight I stopped, my foot halfway up a step.

Someone else was coming down, someone wearing the same kind of military boots. I found the door to the hall, opened it behind me and slipped through. There was a long hall in front of me lined with offices of some kind. I began to run the length of it, trying to reach a turning before the door behind me could open and those exploding slugs tear me in half. The hall seemed endless and I suddenly realized I would never reach the end in time.

I was a rat looking for a hole – and there was none. The doors were locked, all of them, I tried each as I came to it, knowing I would never make it. That stairwell door was opening behind me and the gun was coming up, I didn't dare turn and look but I could feel it. When the door opened under my hand I fell through before I realized what had happened. I locked it behind me and leaned against it in the darkness, panting like a spent animal. Then the light came on and I saw the man sitting behind the desk, smiling at me.

There is a limit to the amount of shock the human body can absorb. I'd had mine. I didn't care if he shot me or offered me a cigarette – I had reached the end of my line. He did neither. He offered me a cigar instead.

'Have one of these, diGriz, I believe they're your brand.'

The body is a slave of habit. Even with death a few inches away it will respond to established custom. My fingers moved of their own volition and took the cigar, my lips clenched it and my lungs sucked it into life. And all the time my eyes watched the man behind the desk waiting for death to reach out.

It must have shown. He waved towards a chair and carefully kept both hands in sight on top of the desk. I still had my gun, it was trained on him.

'Sit down, diGriz, and put that cannon away. If I wanted to kill you, I could have done it a lot easier than herding you into this room.' His eyebrows moved up in surprise when he saw the expression on my face. 'Don't tell me you thought it was an accident that you ended up here?'

I had, up until that moment, and the lack of intelligent reasoning on my part brought on a wave of shame that snapped me back to reality. I had been outwitted and outfought, the least I could do was surrender graciously. I threw the gun on the desk and dropped into the offered chair. He swept the pistol neatly into a drawer and relaxed a bit himself.

'Had me worried there for a minute, the way you stood there rolling your eyes and waving this piece of field artillery around.'

'Who are you?'

He smiled at the abruptness of my tone. 'Well, it doesn't matter who I am. What does matter is the organization that I represent.'

'The Corps?'

'Exactly. The Special Corps. You didn't think I was the local police, did you? They have orders to shoot you on sight. It was only after I told them how to find you that they let the Corps come along on the job. I have some of my men in the building, they're the ones who herded you up here. The rest are all locals with itchy trigger fingers.'

It wasn't very flattering but it was true. I had been pushed around like a class M robot, with every move charted in advance. The old boy behind the desk – for the first time I realized he was about sixty-five – really had my number. The game was over.

'All right, Mr Detective, you have me so there is no sense in gloating. What's next on the program? Psychological reorientation, lobotomy – or just plain firing squad?'

'None of those, I'm afraid. I am here to offer you a job on the Corps.'

The whole thing was so ludicrous that I almost fell out of the chair laughing. Me. James diGriz, the interplanet thief working as a policeman. It was just too funny. He sat patiently, waiting until I was through.

'I will admit it has its ludicrous side – but only at first glance. If you stop to think, you will have to admit that who is better qualified to catch a thief than another thief?'

There was more than a little truth in that, but I wasn't buying my freedom by turning stool pigeon.

'An interesting offer, but I'm not getting out of this by playing the rat. There is even a code among thieves, you know.'

That made him angry. He was bigger than he looked sitting down and the fist he shook in my face was as large as a shoe.

'What kind of stupidity do you call that? It sounds like a line out of a TV thriller. You've never met another crook in your whole life and you know it! And if you did you would cheerfully turn him in if you could make a profit on the deal. The entire essence of your life is individualism – that and the excitement of doing what others can't do. Well that's over now, and you better start admitting it to yourself. You can no longer be the interplanet playboy you used to be – but you *can* do a job that will require every bit of your special talents and abilities. Have you ever killed a man?'

His change of pace caught me off guard, I stumbled out an answer.

'No … not that I know of.'

'Well you haven't, if that will make you sleep any better at night. You're not a homicidal, I checked that on your record before I came out after you. That is why I know you will join the Corps and get a great deal of pleasure out of going after the *other* kind of criminal who is sick, not just socially protesting. The man who can kill and enjoy it.'

He was too convincing, he had all the answers. I had only one more argument and I threw it in with the air of a last ditch defense.

'What about the Corps, if they ever find out you are hiring half-reformed criminals to do your dirty work we will both be shot at dawn.'

This time it was his turn to laugh. I could see nothing funny so I ignored him until he was finished.

'In the first place my boy, *I* am the Corps – at least the man at the top – and what do you think *my* name is? Harold Peters Inskipp, that's what it is!'

'Not the Inskipp that—'

'The same. Inskipp the Uncatchable. The man who looted the Pharsydion II in mid-flight and pulled all those other deals I'm sure you read about in your misspent youth. I was recruited just the way you were.'

He had me on the ropes and knew it. He moved in for the kill.

'And who do you think the rest of our agents are? I don't mean the bright-eyed grads of our technical schools, like the ones on my squad downstairs. I mean the full agents. The men who plan the operations, do the preliminary fieldwork and see that everything comes off smoothly. They're crooks. All crooks. The better they were on their own, the better a job they do for the Corps. It's a great, big, brawling universe and you would be surprised at some of the problems that come up. The only men we can recruit to do the job are the ones who have already succeeded at it.

'Are you on?'

It had happened too fast and I hadn't had time to think. I would probably go on arguing for an hour. But way down in the back of my mind the decision had been made. I was going to do it, I couldn't say no.

I was losing something, and I hoped I wouldn't miss it. No matter what freedom I had working with an organization, I would still be working with other people. The old carefree, sole responsibility days were over. I was joining the ranks of society again.

There was the beginning of a warm feeling at the thought. It would at least be the end of loneliness. Friendship would make up for what I had lost.

CHAPTER

—4—

I have never been more wrong.

The people I met were dull to the point of extinction. They treated me like just another cog going around with the rest of the wheels. I was coggy all right, and kept wondering how I had ever gotten into this mess. Not really wondering, since the memory was still quite vivid. I was carried along with the rest of the gears, their teeth sunk into mine.

We ended up on a planetoid, that much was obvious. But I hadn't the dimmest idea of what planets we were near or even what solar system we were in. Everything was highly secret and hush-hush, as this place was obviously the super-secret headquarters and main base of the Corps School too.

This part I liked. It was the only thing that kept me from cracking out. Dull as the cubes were who taught the courses, the material was something I could really sink my teeth into and shake. I began to see how crude my operations had been. With the gadgetry and techniques I soaked up I could be ten times the crook I had been before. Pushing the thought firmly away helped for a while, but it had a way of sneaking back

31

and whispering nastily in my ear during periods of depression and gloom.

Things went from dull to dead. Half my time was spent working at the files, learning about the number-less successes and few failures of the Corps. I contem-plated cracking out, yet at the same time couldn't help but wonder if this wasn't part of a testing period – to see if I had enough sticktoitiveness to last. I swallowed my temper, muffled my yawns, and took a careful look around. If I couldn't crack out – I could crack *in*. There had to be something I could do to terminate this term of penal servitude.

It wasn't easy – but I found it. By the time I tracked everything down it was well into sleep period. But that was all right. In some ways it even made it more interesting.

When it comes to picking locks and cracking safes I admit to no master. The door to Inskipp's private quarters had an old-fashioned tumbler drum that was easier to pick than my teeth. I must have gone through that door without breaking step. Quiet as I was though, Inskipp still heard me. The light came on and there he was sitting up in bed pointing a .75 caliber recoilless at my sternum.

'You should have more brains than that, diGriz,' he snarled. 'Creeping into my room at night! You could have been shot.'

'No I couldn't,' I told him, as he stowed the cannon back under his pillow. 'A man with a curiosity bump as big as yours will always talk first and shoot later. And besides – none of this pussyfooting around in the dark would be necessary if your screen was open and I could have got a call through.'

Inskipp yawned and poured himself a glass of water

from the dispenser unit above the bed. 'Just because I head the Special Corps, doesn't mean that I *am* the Special Corps,' he said moistly while he drained the glass. 'I have to sleep sometime. My screen is open only for emergency calls, not for every agent who needs his hand held.'

'Meaning I am in the hand-holding category?' I asked with as much sweetness as I could.

'Put yourself in any category you damn well please,' he grumbled as he slumped down in the bed. 'And also put yourself out into the hall and see me tomorrow during working hours.'

He was at my mercy, really. He wanted sleep so much. And he was going to be wide awake so very soon.

'Do you know what this is?' I asked him, poking a large glossy pic under his long broken nose. One eye opened slowly.

'Big warship of some kind, looks like Empire lines. Now for the last time – go away!' he said.

'A very good guess for this late at night,' I told him cheerily. 'It is a late Empire battleship of the Warlord class. Undoubtedly one of the most truly efficient engines of destruction ever manufactured. Over a half mile of defensive screens and armament that could probably turn any fleet existent today into fine radio-active ash—'

'Except for the fact that the last one was broken up for scrap over a thousand years ago,' he mumbled.

I leaned over and put my lips close to his ear. So there would be no chance of misunderstanding. Speaking softly but clearly.

'True, true,' I said. 'But wouldn't you be just a *little*

bit interested if I was to tell you that one is being built today?'

Oh, it was beautiful to watch. The covers went one way and Inskipp went the other. In a single unfolding, concerted motion he left the horizontal and recumbent and stood tensely vertical against the wall. Examining the pic of the battleship under the light. He apparently did not believe in pajama bottoms and it hurt me to see the goose-bumps rising on those thin shanks. But if the legs were thin, the voice was more than full enough to make up for the difference.

'Talk, blast you, diGriz – *talk*!' he roared. 'What is this nonsense about a battleship? Who's building it?'

I had my nail file out and was touching up a cuticle, holding it out for inspection before I said anything. From the corner of my eye I could see him getting purple about the face – but he kept quiet. I savored my small moment of power.

'Put diGriz in charge of the record room for a while, you said, that way he can learn the ropes. Burrowing around in the century-old, dusty files will be just the thing for a free spirit like Slippery Jim diGriz. Teach him discipline. Show him what the Corps stands for. At the same time it will get the records in shape. They have been needing reorganization for quite a while.'

Inskipp opened his mouth, made a choking noise, then closed it. He undoubtedly realized that any interruption would only lengthen my explanation, not shorten it. I smiled and nodded at his decision, then continued.

'So you thought you had me safely out of the way. Breaking my spirit under the guise of "giving me a little background in the Corps" activities.' In this sense your plan failed. Something else happened instead. I nosed through the files and found them most interesting. Particularly the C & M setup – the Categorizer and Memory. That building full of machinery that takes in and digests news and reports from all the planets in the galaxy, indexes it to every category it can possibly relate, then files it. Great machine to work with. I had it digging out spaceship info for me, something I have always been interested in—'

'You should be,' Inskipp interrupted rudely. 'You've stolen enough of them in your time.'

I gave him a hurt look and went on – slowly. 'I won't bore you with all the details, since you seem impatient, but eventually I turned up this plan.' He had it out of my fingers before it cleared my wallet.

'What are you getting it?' he mumbled as he ran his eyes over the blueprints. 'This is an ordinary heavy-cargo and passenger job. It's no more a Warlord battleship than I am.'

It is hard to curl your lips with contempt and talk at the same time, but I succeeded. 'Of course. You don't expect them to file warship plans with the League Registry, do you? But, as I said, I know more than a little bit about ships. It seemed to me this thing was just too big for the use intended. Enough old ships are fuel-wasters, you don't have to build new ones to do that. This started me thinking and I punched for a complete list of ships that size that had been constructed in the past. You can imagine my surprise when, after three minutes of groaning, the C & M only produced six. One was built for self-sustaining colony attempt at the second galaxy. For all we know she is still on the way. The other five were all D-class colonizers, built during the Expansion when large populations were moved. Too big to be practical now.

'I was still teased, and I had no idea what a ship this large could be used for. So I removed the time interlock on the C & M and let it pick around through the entire history of space to see if it could find a comparison. It sure did. Right at the Golden Age of Empire expansion, the giant Warlord battleship. The machine even found a blueprint for me.'

Inskipp grabbed again and began comparing the two prints. I leaned over his shoulder and pointed out the interesting parts.

'Notice – if the engine room specs are changed slightly to include cargo hold, there is plenty of room for the brutes needed. This superstructure – obviously just tacked onto the plans – gets thrown away, and turrets take its place. The hulls are identical. A change here, a shift there, and the stodgy freighter becomes the fast battlewagon. These changes could be made during construction, then plans filed. By the time anyone in the League found out what was being built the ship would be finished and launched. Of course, this could all be coincidence – the plans of a newly built ship agreeing to six places with those of a ship being built a thousand years ago. But if you think so, I will give you hundred-to-one odds you are wrong, any size bet you name.'

I wasn't winning any sucker bets that night. Inskipp had led just as crooked a youth as I had, and needed no help in smelling a fishy deal. While he pulled on his clothes he shot questions at me.

'And the name of the peace-loving planet that is building this bad-memory from the past?'

'Cittanuvo. Second planet of a B star in Corona Borealis. No other colonized planets in the system.'

'Never heard of it,' Inskipp said as we took the private drop chute to his office. 'Which may be a good or a bad sign. Wouldn't be the first time trouble came from some out-of-the-way spot I never even knew existed.'

With the automatic disregard for others of the truly dedicated, he pressed the scramble button on his desk. Very quickly sleepy-eyed clerks and assistants were bringing files and records. We went through them together.

Modesty prevented me from speaking first, but I had a very short wait before Inskipp reached the same conclusion I had. He hurled a folder the length of the room and scowled out at the harsh dawn light.

'The more I look at this thing,' he said, 'the fishier it gets. This planet seems to have no possible motive or use for a battleship. But they are building one – *that* I will swear on a stack of one thousand credit notes as high as this building. Yet what will they do with it when they have it built? They have an expanding culture, no unemployment, a surplus of heavy metals and ready markets for all they produce. No hereditary enemies, feuds or the like. If it wasn't for this battleship thing, I would call them an ideal League planet. I have to know more about them.'

'I've already called the spaceport – in your name of course,' I told him. 'Ordered a fast courier ship. I'll leave within the hour.'

'Aren't you getting a little ahead of yourself, diGriz,' he said. Voice chill as the icecap. 'I still give the orders and I'll tell you when you're ready for an independent command.'

I was sweetness and light because a lot depended on his decision. 'Just trying to help, chief, get things ready in case you wanted more info. And this isn't really an operation, just a reconnaissance. I can do that as well as any of the experienced operators. And it may give me the experience I need, so that some day I, too, will be qualified to join the ranks ...'

'All right,' he said. 'Stop shoveling it on while I can still breathe. Get out there. Find out what is happening. Then get back. Nothing else – and that's an order.'

By the way he said it, I knew he thought there was little chance of its happening that way. And he was right.

CHAPTER

— 5 —

A quick stop at supply and record sections gave me everything I needed. The sun was barely clear of the horizon when the silver barb of my ship lifted in the gray field, then blasted into space.

The trip only took a few days, more than enough time to memorize everything I needed to know about Cittanuvo. And the more I knew the less I could understand their need for a battleship. It didn't fit. Cittanuvo was a secondary settlement out of the Cellini system, and I had run into these settlements before. They were all united in a loose alliance and bickered a lot among themselves, but never came to blows. If anything, they shared a universal abhorrence of war.

Yet they were secretly building a battleship.

Since I was only chasing my tail with this line of thought, I put it out of my mind and worked on some tri-di chess problems. This filled the time until Cittanuvo blinked into the bow screen.

One of my most effective mottoes has always been, 'Secrecy can be an obviousity.' What the magicians call misdirection. Let people very obviously see what you want them to see, then they'll never notice what is hidden. This was why I landed at midday, on the largest field on the planet, after a very showy approach. I was already dressed for my role, and out of the ship before the landing braces stopped vibrating. Buckling the fur cape around my shoulders with the platinum clasp, I stamped down the ramp. The sturdy little M-3 robot rumbled after me with my bags. Heading directly towards the main gate, I ignored the scurry of activity around the customs building. Only when a uniformed under-official of some kind ran over to me, did I give the field any attention.

Before he could talk I did, foot in the door and stay on top.

'Beautiful planet you have here. Delightful climate! Ideal spot for a country home. Friendly people, always willing to help strangers and all that I imagine. That's what I like. Makes me feel grateful. Very pleased to meet you. I am the Grand Duke Sant' Angelo.' I shook his hand enthusiastically at this point and let a one hundred credit note slip into his palm.

'Now,' I added, 'I wonder if you would ask the customs agents to look at my bags here. Don't want to waste time, do we? The ship is open, they can check that whenever they please.'

My manner, clothes, jewelry, the easy way I passed money around and the luxurious sheen of my bags, could mean only one thing. There was little that was worth smuggling into or out of Cittanuvo. Certainly nothing a rich man would be interested in. The official murmured something with a smile, spoke a few words into his phone, and the job was done.

A small wave of customs men hung stickers on my luggage, peeked into one or two for conformity's sake, and waved me through. I shook hands all around – a rustling handclasp of course – then was on my way. A cab was summoned, a hotel suggested. I nodded agreement and settled back while the robot loaded the bags about me.

The ship was completely clean. Everything I might need for the job was in my luggage. Some of it quite lethal and explosive, and very embarrassing if it were discovered in my bags. In the safety of my hotel suite I made a change of clothes and personality. After the robot had checked the rooms for bugs.

And very nice gadgets too, these Corps robots. It looked and acted like a moron M-3 all the time. It was anything but. The brain was as good as any other robot brain I have known, plus the fact that the chunky body was crammed with devices and machines of varying use. It chugged slowly around the room, moving my bags and laying out my kit. And all the time following a careful route that covered every inch of the suite. When it had finished it stopped and called the all-clear.

'All rooms checked. Results negative except for one optic bug in that wall.'

'Should you be pointing like that?' I asked the robot. 'Might make people suspicious, you know.'

'Impossible,' the robot said with mechanical surety. 'I brushed against it and it is now unserviceable.'

With this assurance I pulled off my flashy clothes and slipped into the midnight black dress uniform of an admiral in the League Grand Fleet. It came complete with decorations, gold bullion, and all the necessary documents. I thought it a little showy myself, but it was just the thing to make the right impression on Cittanuvo. Like many other planets, this one was uniform-conscious. Delivery boys, street cleaners, clerks – all had to have characteristic uniforms. Much prestige attached to them, and my black dress outfit should rate as high as any uniform in the galaxy.

A long cloak would conceal the uniform while I left the hotel, but the gold-encrusted helmet and a brief case of papers were a problem. I had never explored all the possibilities of the pseudo M-3 robot, perhaps it could be of help.

'You there, short and chunky,' I called. 'Do you have any concealed compartments or drawers built into your steel hide? If so, let's see.'

For a second I thought the robot exploded. The thing had more drawers in it than a battery of cash registers. Big, small, flat, thin, they shot out on all sides. One held a gun and two more were stuffed with grenades; the rest were empty. I put the hat in one, the brief case in another and snapped my fingers. The drawers slid shut and its metal hide was as smooth as ever.

I pulled on a fancy sports cap, buckled the cape up tight, and was ready to go. The luggage was all booby-trapped and could defend itself. Guns, gas, poison needles, the usual sort of thing. In the last resort it would blow itself up. The M-3 went down by a freight elevator. I used a back stairs and we met in the street.

Since it was still daylight I didn't take a heli, but rented a groundcar instead. We had a leisurely drive out into the country and reached President Ferraro's house after dark.

As befitted the top official of a rich planet, the place was a mansion. But the security precautions were ludicrous to say the least. I took myself and a three hundred fifty kilo robot through the guards and alarms without causing the slightest stir. President Ferraro, a bachelor, was eating his dinner. This gave me enough undisturbed time to search his study.

There was absolutely nothing. Nothing to do with wars or battleships that is. If I had been interested in blackmail I had enough evidence in my hand to support me for life. I was looking for something bigger than political corruption, however.

When Ferraro rolled into his study after dinner the room was dark. I heard him murmur something about the servants and fumble for the switch. Before he found it, the robot closed the door and turned on the lights. I sat behind his desk, all his personal papers before me – weighted down with a pistol – and as fierce a scowl as I could raise smeared across my face. Before he got over the shock I snapped an order at him.

'Come over here and sit down, *quick!*'

The robot hustled him across the room at the same time, so he had no choice except to obey. When he saw the papers on the desk his eyes bulged and he just gurgled a little. Before he could recover I threw a thick folder in front of him.

'I am Admiral Thar, League Grand Fleet. These are my credentials. You had better check them.' Since they were as good an any real admiral's I didn't worry in the slightest. Ferraro went through them as carefully as he could in his rattled state, even checking the seals under UV. It gave him time to regain a bit of control and he used it to bluster.

'What do you mean by entering my private quarters and burglaring—'

'You're in very bad trouble,' I said in as gloomy a voice as I could muster.

Ferraro's tanned face went a dirty gray at my words. I pressed the advantage.

'I am arresting you for conspiracy, extortion, theft, and whatever other charges develop after a careful review of these documents. Seize him.' This last order was directed at the robot who was well briefed in its role. It rumbled forward and locked its hand around Ferraro's wrist, handcuff style. He barely noticed.

'I can explain,' he said desperately. 'Everything can be explained. There is no need to make such charges. I don't know what papers you have there, so I wouldn't attempt to say they are all forgeries. I have many enemies you know. If the League knew the difficulties faced on a backward planet like this ...'

'That will be entirely enough,' I snapped, cutting him off with a wave of my hand. 'All of those questions will be answered by a court at the proper time. There is only one question I want an answer to now. Why are you building a battleship?'

The man was a great actor. His eyes opened wide, his jaw dropped, he sank back into the chair as if he had been tapped lightly with a hammer. When he managed to speak the words were completely unnecessary; he had already registered every evidence of injured innocence.

'What battleship?' he gasped.

'The Warlord class battleship that is being built at the Cenerentola Spaceyards. Disguised behind these blueprints.' I threw them across the desk to him, and pointed to the one corner. 'Those are your initials there, authorizing construction.'

Ferraro still had the baffled act going as he fumbled with the papers, examined the initials and such. I gave

44

him plenty of time. He finally put them down, shaking his head.

'I know nothing about any battleship. These are the plans for a new cargo liner. Those are my initials, I recall putting them there.'

I phrased my question carefully, as I had him right where I wanted him now. 'You deny any knowledge of the Warlord battleship that is being built from these modified plans.'

'These are the plans for an ordinary passenger-freighter, that is all I know.'

His words had the simple innocence of a young child's. Was he ever caught. I sat back with a relaxed sigh and lit a cigar.

'Wouldn't you be interested in knowing something about that robot who is holding you,' I said. He looked down, as if aware for the first time that the robot had been holding him by the wrist during the interview. 'That is no ordinary robot. It has a number of interesting devices built into its fingertips. Thermo-couples, galvanometers, things like that. While you talked it registered your skin temperature, blood pressure, amount of perspiration and such. In other words it is an efficient and fast working lie detector. We will now hear all about your lies.'

Ferraro pulled away from the robot's hand as if it had been a poisonous snake. I blew a relaxed smoke ring. 'Report,' I said to the robot. 'Has this man told any lies?'

'Many,' the robot said. 'Exactly seventy-four per cent of all statements he made were false.'

'Very good,' I nodded, throwing the last lock on my trap. 'That means he knows all about this battleship.'

'The subject has no knowledge of the battleship,' the

robot said coldly. 'All of his statements concerning the construction of this ship were true.'

Now it was my turn for the gaping and eye-popping act while Ferraro pulled himself together. He had no idea I wasn't interested in his other hanky-panky, but could tell I had had a low blow. It took an effort, but I managed to get my mind back into gear and consider the evidence.

If President Ferraro didn't know about the battleship, he must have been taken in by the cover-up job. But if he wasn't responsible – who was? Some militaristic clique that meant to overthrow him and take power? I didn't know enough about the planet, so I enlisted Ferraro on my side.

This was easy – even without the threat of exposure of the documents I had found in his files. Using their disclosure as a prod I could have made him jump through hoops. It wasn't necessary. As soon as I showed him the different blueprints and explained the possibilities he understood. If anything, he was more eager than I was to find out who was using his administration as a cat's-paw. By silent agreement the documents were forgotten.

We agreed that the next logical step would be the Cenerentola Spaceyards. He had some idea of sniffing around quietly first, trying to get a line to his political opponents. I gave him to understand that the League, and the League Navy in particular, wanted to stop the construction of the battleship. After that he could play his politics. With this point understood he called his car and squadron of guards and we made a parade to the shipyards. It was a four-hour drive and we made plans on the way down.

*

The spaceyard manager was named Rocca, and he was happily asleep when we arrived. But not for long. The parade of uniforms and guns in the middle of the night had him frightened into a state where he could hardly walk. I imagine he was as full of petty larceny as Ferraro. No innocent man could have looked so terror stricken. Taking advantage of the situation, I latched my motorized lie detector onto him and began snapping the questions.

Even before I had all the answers I began to get the drift of things. They were a little frightening, too. The manager of the spaceyard that was building the ship had no idea of its true nature.

Anyone with less self-esteem than myself – or who had led a more honest early life – might have doubted his own reasoning at that moment. I didn't. The ship on the ways *still* resembled a warship to six places. And knowing human nature the way I do, that was too much of a coincidence to expect. Occam's razor always points the way. If there are two choices to take, take the simpler. In this case I chose the natural acquisitive instinct of man as opposed to blind chance and accident. Nevertheless I put the theory to the test.

Looking over the original blueprints again, the big superstructure hit my eye. In order to turn the ship into a warship that would have to be one of the first things to go.

'Rocca!' I barked, in what I hoped was authentic old space-dog manner. 'Look at these plans, at this space-going front porch here. Is it still being built onto the ship?'

He shook his head at once and said, 'No, the plans were changed. We had to fit in some kind of new

47

meteor-repelling gear for operating in the planetary debris belt.'

I flipped through my case and drew out a plan. 'Does your new gear look anything like this?' I asked, throwing it across the table to him.

He rubbed his jaw while he looked at it. 'Well,' he said hesitatingly, 'I don't want to say for certain. After all, these details aren't in my department, I'm just responsible for final assembly, not unit work. But this surely looks like the thing they installed. Big thing. Lots of power leads—'

It was a battleship all right, no doubt of that now. I was mentally reaching around to pat myself on the back when the meaning of his words sank in.

'Installed!' I shouted. 'Did you say installed?'

Rocca collapsed away from my roar and gnawed his nails. 'Yes –' he said, 'not too long ago. I remember there was some trouble ...'

'And what else?' I interrupted him. Cold moisture was beginning to collect along my spine now. 'The drives, controls – are they in, too?'

'Why, yes,' he said. 'How did you know? The normal scheduling was changed around, causing a great deal of unnecessary trouble.'

The cold sweat was now a running river of fear. I was beginning to have the feeling that I had been missing the boat all along the line. The original estimated date of completion was nearly a year away. But there was no real reason why that couldn't be changed, too.

'Cars! Guns!' I bellowed. 'To the spaceyard. If that ship is anywhere near completion, we are in big, *big* trouble!'

All the bored guards had a great time with the sirens, lights, accelerators on the floor and that sort of thing. We blasted a screaming hole through the night right to the spaceyard and through the gate.

It didn't make any difference, we were still too late. A uniformed watchman frantically waved to us and the whole convoy jerked to a stop.

The ship was gone.

Rocca couldn't believe it, neither could the president. They wandered up and down the empty ways where it had been built. I just crunched down in the back of the car, chewing my cigar to pieces and cursing myself for being a fool.

I had missed the obvious fact, being carried away by the thought of a planetary government building a warship. The government was involved for sure – but only as a pawn. No little planet-bound political mind could have dreamed up as big a scheme as this. I smelled a rat – a stainless steel one. Someone who operated the way I had done before my conversion.

Now that the rodent was well out of the bag I knew just where to look, and had a pretty good idea of what I would find. Rocca, the spaceyard manager, had staggered back and was pulling at his hair, cursing and crying at the same time. President Ferraro had his gun out and was staring at it grimly. It was hard to tell if he was thinking of murder or suicide. I didn't care which. All he had to worry about was the next election, when the voters and the political competition would carve him up for losing the ship. My troubles were a little bigger.

I had to find the battleship before it blasted its way across the galaxy.

'Rocca!' I shouted. 'Get into the car. I want to see

49

your records – *all* of your records – and I want to see them right now.'

He climbed wearily in and had directed the driver before he fully realized what was happening. Blinking at the sickly light of dawn brought him slowly back to reality.

'But admiral ... the hour! Everyone will be asleep ...'

I just growled, but it was enough. Rocca caught the idea from my expression and grabbed the car phone. The office doors were open when we got there.

Normally I curse the paper tangles of bureaucracy, but this was one time when I blessed them all. These people had it down to a fine science. Not a rivet fell, but that its fall was noted – in quintuplicate. And later followed up with a memo, *rivet, wastage, query*. The facts I needed were all neatly tucked away in their paper catacombs. All I had to do was sniff them out. I didn't try to look for first causes, this would have taken too long. Instead I concentrated my attention on the recent modifications, like the gun turret, that would quickly give me a trail to the guilty parties.

Once the clerks understood what I had in mind they hurled themselves into their work, urged on by the fires of patriotism and the burning voices of their superiors. All I had to do was suggest a line of search and the relevant documents would begin appearing at once.

Bit by bit a pattern started to emerge. A delicate webwork of forgery, bribery, chicanery and falsehood. It could only have been conceived by a mind as brilliantly crooked as my own. I chewed my lip with jealousy. Like all great ideas, this one was basically simple.

A party or parties unknown had neatly warped the ship construction program to their own ends. Undoubtedly they had started the program for the giant transport, that would have to be checked later. And once the program was underway, it had been guided with a skill that bordered on genius. Orders were originated in many places, passed on, changed and shuffled. I painfully traced each one to its source. Many times the source was a forgery. Some changes seemed to be unexplainable, until I noticed the officers in question had a temporary secretary while their normal assistants were ill. All the girls had had food poisoning, a regular epidemic it seemed. Each of them in turn had been replaced by the same girl. She stayed just long enough in each position to see that the battleship plan moved forward one more notch.

This girl was obviously the assistant to the Master-mind who originated the scheme. He sat in the center of the plot, like a spider on its web, pulling the strings that set things into motion. My first thought that a gang was involved proved wrong. All my secondary suspects turned out to be simple forgeries, not individuals. In the few cases where forgery wasn't adequate, my mysterious X had apparently hired himself to do the job. X himself had the permanent job of Assistant Engineering Designer. One by one the untangled threads ran to this office. He also had a secretary whose 'illnesses' coincided with her employment in other offices.

When I straightened up from my desk the ache in my back stabbed like a hot wire. I swallowed a painkiller and looked around at my drooping, sack-eyed assistants who had shared the sleepless seventy-two hour task. They sat or slumped against the furniture, waiting for my conclusion. Even President Ferraro was there, his hair looking scraggly where he had pulled out handfuls.

'You've found them, the criminal ring?' he asked, his fingers groping over his scalp for a fresh hold.

'I have found them, yes,' I said hoarsely. 'But not a criminal ring. An inspired master criminal – who apparently has more executive ability in one ear lobe than all your bribe-bloated bureaucrats – and his female assistant. They pulled the entire job by themselves. His name, or undoubtedly pseudoname, is Pepe Nero. The girl is called Angelina ...'

'Arrest them at once! Guards ... guards –' Ferraro's voice died away as he ran out of the room. I talked to his vanishing back.

'That is just what we intend to do, but it's a little difficult at the moment since they are the ones who not only built the battleship, but undoubtedly stole it as well. It was fully automated so no crew is necessary.'

'What do you plan to do?' one of the clerks asked.

'I shall do nothing,' I told him, with the snapped precision of an old space veteran. 'The League fleet is already closing in on the renegades and you will be informed of the capture. Thank you for your assistance.'

CHAPTER

— 6 —

I threw them as snappy a salute as I could muster and
they filed out. Staring gloomily at their backs I envied
for one moment their simple faith in the League Navy.
When in reality the vengeful fleet was just as imaginary
as my admiral's rating. This was still a job for the
Corps. Inskipp would have to be given the latest
information at once. I had sent him a psigram about
the theft, but there was no answer as yet. Maybe the
identity of the thieves would stir some response out of
him.

My message was in code, but it could be quickly
broken if someone wanted to try hard enough. I took it
to the message center myself. The psiman was in his
transparent cubicle and I locked myself in with him.
His eyes were unfocused as he spoke softly into a mike,
pulling in a message from somewhere across the
galaxy. Outside the rushing transcribers copied, coded
and filed messages, but no sound penetrated the
insulated wall. I waited until his attention clicked back
into the room, and handed him the sheets of paper.

'League Central 14 – rush,' I told him.

He raised his eyebrows, but didn't ask any questions. Establishing contact only took a few seconds, as

they had an entire battery of psimen for their communications. He read the code words carefully, shaping them with his mouth but not speaking aloud, the power of his thoughts carrying across the light-years of distance. As soon as he was finished I took back the sheet, tore it up and pocketed the pieces.

I had my answer back quickly enough, Inskipp must have been hovering around waiting for my message. The mike was turned off to the transcribers outside, and I took the code groups down in shorthand myself.

'... xybb dfil fdno, and if you don't – don't come back!'

The message broke into clear at the end and the psiman smiled as he spoke the words. I broke the point off my stylus and growled at him not to repeat *any* of this message, as it was classified, and I would personally see him shot if he did. That got rid of the smile, but didn't make me feel any better.

The decoded message turned out not to be as bad as I had imagined. Until further notice I was in charge of tracking and capturing the stolen battleship. I could call on the League for any aid I needed. I would keep my identity as an admiral for the rest of the job. I was to keep him informed of progress. Only those ominous last words in clear kept my happiness from being complete.

I had been handed my long-awaited assignment. But translated into simple terms my orders were to get the battleship, or it would be my neck. Never a word about my efforts in uncovering the plot in the first place. This is a heartless world we live in.

This moment of self-pity relaxed me and I immediately went to bed. Since my main job now was waiting, I could wait just as well sleep.

*

And waiting was all I could do. Of course there were secondary tasks such as ordering a Naval cruiser for my own use, and digging for more information on the thieves, but these really were secondary to my main purpose. Which was waiting for bad news. There was no place I could go that would be better situated for the chase than Cittanuvo. The missing ship could have gone in any direction. With each passing minute the sphere of probable locations grew larger by the power of the squared cube. I kept the on-watch crew of the cruiser at duty stations and confined the rest within a one hundred yard radius of the ship.

There was little more information on Pepe and Angelina, they had covered their tracks well. Their backgrounds were unknown, though the fact they both talked with a slight accent suggested an off-world origin. There was one dim picture of Pepe, chubby but looking too grim to be a happy fat boy. There was no picture of the girl. I shuffled the meager findings, controlled my impatience, and kept the ship's psiman busy pulling in all the reports of any kind of trouble in space. The navigator and I plotted their locations in his tank, comparing the positions in relation to the growing sphere that enclosed all the possible locations of the stolen ship. Some of the disasters and apparent accidents hit inside this area, but further investigation proved them all to have natural causes.

I had left standing orders that all reports falling inside the danger area were to be brought to me at any time. The messenger woke me from a deep sleep, turning on the light and handing me the slip of paper. I blinked myself awake, read the first two lines, and pressed the *action station* alarm over my bunk. I'll say this, the Navy boys know their business. When the sirens screamed, the crew secured ship and blasted off before I had finished reading the report. As soon as my eyeballs unsquashed back into focus I read it through, then once more carefully from the beginning.

It looked like the one we had been waiting for. There were no witnesses to the tragedy, but a number of monitor stations had picked up the discharge static of a large energy weapon being fired. Triangulation had lead investigators to the spot where they found a freighter, *Ogget's Dream*, with a hole punched through it as big as a railroad tunnel. The freighter's cargo of plutonium was gone.

I read *Pepe* in every line of the message. Since he was flying an undermanned battleship, he had used it in the most efficient way possible. If he attempted to negotiate or threaten another ship, the element of chance would be introduced. So he had simply roared up to the unsuspecting freighter and blasted her with the monster guns his battleship packed. All eighteen men aboard had been killed instantly. The thieves were also murderers.

I was under pressure now to act. And under a greater pressure not to make any mistakes. Roly-poly Pepe had shown himself to be a ruthless killer. He knew what he wanted – then reached out and took it. Destroying anyone who stood in his way. More people would die before this was over, it was up to me to keep that number as small as possible.

Ideally I should have rushed out the fleet with guns blazing and dragged him to justice. Very nice, and I wished it could be done that way. Except where was he? A battleship may be gigantic on some terms of reference, but in the immensity of the galaxy it is microscopically infinitesimal. As long as it stayed out of the regular lanes of commerce, and clear of detector stations and planets, it would never be found.

Then how *could* I find it – and having found it, catch it? When the infernal thing was more than a match for any ship it might meet. That was my problem. It had kept me awake nights and talking to myself days, since there was no easy answer.

I had to construct a solution, slowly and carefully. Since I couldn't be sure where Pepe was going to be next, I had to make him go where I wanted him to.

There were some things in my favor. The most important was the fact I had forced him to make his play before he was absolutely ready. It wasn't chance that he had left the same day I arrived on Cittanuvo. Any plan as elaborate as his certainly included warning of approaching danger. The drive on the battleship, as well as controls and primary armament had been installed weeks before I showed up. Much of the subsidiary work remained to be done when the ship had left. One witness of the theft had graphically described the power lines and cables dangling from the ship's locks when she lifted.

My arrival had forced Pepe off balance. Now I had to keep pushing until he fell. This meant I had to think as he did, fall into his plan, think ahead – then trap him. Set a thief to catch a thief. A great theory, only I felt uncomfortably on the spot when I tried to put it into practice.

A drink helped, as did a cigar. Puffing on it, staring at the smooth bulkhead, relaxed me a bit. After all – there aren't that many things you can do with a battleship. You can't run a big con, blow safes or make burmedex with it. It is hell-on-jets for space piracy, but that's about all.

'Great, great – but why a battleship?'

I was talking to myself, normally a bad sign, but right now I didn't care. The mood of space piracy had seized me and I had been going along fine. Until this glaring inconsistency jumped out and hit me square in the eye.

Why a battleship? Why all the trouble and years of work to get a ship that two people could just barely manage? With a tenth of the effort Pepe could have had a cruiser that would have suited his purposes just as well.

Just as good for space piracy, that is – but not for *his* purposes. He had wanted a battleship, and he had gotten himself a battleship. Which meant he had more in mind than simple piracy. What? It was obvious that Pepe was a monomaniac, an egomaniac, and as psychotic as a shorted computer. Some day the mystery of how he had slipped through the screen of official testing would have to be investigated. That wasn't my concern now. He still had to be caught.

A plan was beginning to take shape in my head, but I didn't rush it. First I had to be sure that I knew him well. Any man that can con an entire world into building a battleship for him – then steal it from them – is not going to stop there. The ship would need a crew, a base for refueling and a mission.

Fuel had been taken care of first, the gutted hull of *Ogget's Dream* was silent witness to that. There were countless planets that could be used as a base. Getting a crew would be more difficult in these peaceful times, although I could think of a few answers to that one, too. Raid the mental hospitals and jails. Do that often enough and you would have a crew that would make any private chief proud. Though piracy was, of course, too mean an ambition to ascribe to this boy. Did he want to rule a whole planet – or maybe an entire system? Or more? I shuddered a bit as the thought hit me. Was there really anything that could stop a plan like this once it got rolling? During the Kingly Wars any number of types with a couple of ships and less brains than Pepe had set up just this kind of empire. They were all pulled down in the end, since their success depended on one-man rule. But the price tht had to be paid first!

This was the plan and I felt in my bones that I was right. I might be wrong on some of the minor details, they weren't important. I knew the general outline of the idea, just as when I bumped into a mark I knew how much he could be taken for, and just how to do it. There are natural laws in crime as in every other field of human endeavor. I *knew* this was it.

'Get the Communications Officer in here at once,' I shouted at the intercom. 'Also a couple of clerks with transcribers. And fast – this is a matter of life or death!' This last had a hollow ring, and I realized my enthusiasm had carried me out of character. I buttoned my collar, straightened my ribbons and squared my shoulders. By the time they knocked on the door I was all admiral again.

Acting on my orders the ship dropped out of warpdrive so our psiman could get through to the other operators. Captain Steng grumbled as we floated there with the engines silent, wasting precious days, while half his crew was involved in getting out what appeared to be insane instructions. My plan was beyond his understanding. Which is, of course, why he is a captain and I'm an admiral, even a temporary one.

Following my orders, the navigator again constructed a sphere of speculation in his tank. The surface of the sphere contacted all the star systems a day's flight ahead of the maximum flight of the stolen battleship. There weren't too many of these at first and the psiman could handle them all, calling each in turn and sending news releases to the Naval Public Relations officers there. As the sphere kept growing he started to drop behind, steadily losing ground. By this time I had a general release prepared, along with directions for use and follow up, which he sent to Central 14. The battery of psimen there contacted the individual planets and all we had to do was keep adding to the list of planets.

The release and follow-ups all harped on one theme. I expanded on it, waxed enthusiastic, condemned it, and worked it into an interview. I wrote as many variations as I could, so it could be slipped into as many different formats as possible. In one form or another I wanted the basic information in every magazine, newspaper and journal inside that expanding sphere.

'What in the devil does this nonsense *mean*?' Captain Steng asked peevishly. He had long since given up the entire operation as a futile one, and spent most of the time in his cabin worrying about the effect of it on his service record. Boredom or curiosity had driven him out, and he was reading one of my releases with horror.

'Billionaire to found own world ... space yacht filled with luxuries to last a hundred years,' the captain's face grew red as he flipped through the stack of notes.

'What connection does this tripe have with catching those murderers?'

When we were alone he was anything but courteous to me, having assured himself by not-too-subtle questioning that I was a curious admiral. There was no doubt I was still in charge, but our relationship was anything but formal.

'This tripe and nonsense,' I told him, 'is the bait tht will snag our fish. A trap for Pepe and his partner in crime.'

'Who is this mysterious billionaire?'

'Me,' I said. 'I've always wanted to be rich.'

'But this ship, the space yacht, where is it?'

'Being built now in the naval shipyard at Udrydde. We're almost ready to go there now, soon as this batch of instructions goes out.'

Captain Steng dropped the releases onto the table, then carefully wiped his hands off to remove any possible infection. He was trying to be fair and considerate of my views, and not succeeding in the slightest.

'It doesn't make sense,' he growled. 'How can you be sure this killer will ever read one of these things? And if he does – why should he be interested? It looks to me as if you are wasting time while he slips through your fingers. The alarm should be out and every ship notified. The Navy alerted and patrols set on all spacelanes—'

'Which he could easily avoid by going around, or better yet not even bother about, since he can lick any ship we have. That's not the answer,' I told him. 'This Pepe is smart and as tricky as a fixed gambling machine. That's his strength – and his weakness as well. Characters like that never think it possible for someone else to outthink them. Which is what *I'm* going to do.'

'Modest, aren't you,' Steng said.

'I try not to be,' I told him. 'False modesty is the refuge of the incompetent. I'm going to catch this thug and I'll tell you how I'll do it. He's going to hit again soon, and wherever he hits there will be some kind of a periodical with my plant in it. Whatever else he is after, he is going to take all of the magazines and papers he can find. Partly to satisfy his own ego, but mostly to keep track of the things he is interested in. Such as ship sailings.'

'You're just guessing – you don't know all this.'

His automatic assumption of my incompetence was beginning to get me annoyed. I bridled my temper and tried one last time.

'Yes, I'm guessing – an informed guess – but I do know some facts as well. *Ogget's Dream* was cleaned out of all reading matter, that was one of the first things I checked. We can't stop the battleship from attacking again, but we can see to it that the time after that she sails into a trap.'

'I don't know,' the captain said, 'it sounds to me like ...'

I never heard what it sounded like, which is all right since he was getting under my skin and I might have been tempted to pull my pseudo-rank. The alarm sirens cut his sentence off and we foot-raced to the communications room.

Captain Steng won by a nose, it was his ship and he knew all the shortcuts. The psiman was holding out a transcription, but he summed it up in one sentence. He looked at me while he talked and his face was hard and cold.

'They hit again, knocked out a Navy supply satellite, thirty-four men dead.'

'If your plan doesn't work, *admiral*,' the captain whispered hoarsely in my ear, 'I'll personally see that you're flayed alive!'

'If my plan doesn't work, *captain* – there won't be enough of my skin left to pick up with a tweezer. Now if you please, I'd like to get to Udrydde and board my ship as soon as possible.'

The easy-going hatred and contempt of all my associates had annoyed me, thrown me off balance. I was thinking with anger now, not with logic. Forcing a bit of control, I ordered my thoughts, checking off a mental list.

'Belay that last command,' I shouted, getting back into my old space-dog mood. 'Get a call through first and find out if any of our plants were picked up during the raid.'

While the psiman unfocused his eyes and mumbled under his breath I riffled some papers, relaxed and cool. The ratings and officers waited tensely, and made some slight attempt to conceal their hatred of me. It took about ten minutes to get an answer.

'Affirmative,' the psiman said. 'A store ship docked there twenty hours before the attack. Among other things, it left newspapers containing the article.'

'Very good,' I said calmly. 'Send a general order to suspend all future activity with the planted releases. Send it by psimen only, no mention on any other Naval signaling equipment, there's a good chance now it might be "overheard".'

I strolled out slowly, in command of the situation.

Keeping my face turned away so they couldn't see the cold sweat.

It was a fast run to Udrydde where my billionaire's yacht, the *Eldorado*, was waiting. The dockyard commander showed me the ship, and made a noble effort to control his curiosity. I took a sadistic revenge on the Navy by not telling him a word about my mission. After checking out the controls and special apparatus with the technicians, I cleared the ship. There was a tape in the automatic navigator that would put me on the course mentioned in all the articles, just a press of a button and I would be on my way. I pressed the button.

It was a beautiful ship, and the dockyard had been lavish with their attention to detail. From bow to rear tubes she was plated in pure gold. There are other metals with a higher albedo, but none that give a richer effect. All the fittings, inside and out, were either machine-turned or plated. All this work could not have been done in the time allotted, the Navy must have adapted a luxury yacht to my needs.

Everything was ready. Either Pepe would make his move – or I would sail on to my billionaire's paradise planet. It that happened, it would be best if I stayed there.

Now that I was in space, past the point of no return, all the doubts that I had dismissed fought for attention. The plan that had seemed so clear and logical now began to look like a patched and crazy makeshift.

'Hold on there, sailor,' I said to myself. Using my best admiral's voice. 'Nothing has changed. It's still the best and *only* plan possible under the circumstances.'

Was it? Could I be sure that Pepe, flying his

mountain of a ship and eating Navy rations, would be interested in some of the comforts and luxuries of life? Or if the luxuries didn't catch his eye, would he be interested in the planetary homesteading gear? I had loaded the cards with all the things he might want, and planted the information where he could get it. He had the bait now – but would he grab the hook?

I couldn't tell. And I could work myself into a neurotic state if I kept running through the worry cycle. It took an effort to concentrate on anything else, but it had to be made. The next four days passed very slowly.

CHAPTER

— 7 —

When the alarm blew off, all I felt was an intense sensation of relief. I might be dead and blasted to dust in the next few minutes, but that didn't seem to make much difference.

Pepe had swallowed the bait. There was only one ship in the galaxy that could knock back a blip that big at such a distance. It was closing fast, using the raw energy of the battleship engines for a headlong approach. My ship bucked a bit as the tug-beams locked on at maximum distance. The radio bleeped at me for attention at the same time. I waited as long as I dared, then flipped it on. The voice boomed out.

'... That you are under the guns of a warship! Don't attempt to run, signal, take evasive action, or in any other way ...'

'Who are you – and what the devil do you want?' I spluttered into the mike. I had my scanner on, so they could see me, but my own screen stayed dark. They weren't sending any picture. In a way it made my act easier, I just played to an unseen audience. They could see the rich cut of my clothes, the luxurious cabin behind me. Of course they couldn't see my hands.

'It doesn't matter who we are,' the radio boomed

again. 'Just obey orders if you care to live. Stay away from the controls until we have tied on, then do exactly as I say.'

There were two distant clangs as magnetic grapples hit the hull. A little later the ship lurched, drawn home against the battleship. I let my eyes roll in fear, looking around for a way to escape – and taking a peek at the outside scanners. The yacht was flush against the spacefilling bulk of the other ship. I pressed the button that sent the torch-wielding robot on his way.

'Now let me tell you something,' I snapped into the mike, wiping away the worried billionaire expression. 'First I'll repeat your own warning – obey orders if you want to live. I'll show you why—'

When I threw the big switch a carefully worked out sequence took place. First, of course, the hull was magnetized and the bombs fused. A light blinked as the scanner in the cabin turned off, and the one in the generator room came on. I checked the monitor screen to make sure, then started into the spacesuit. It had to be done fast, at the same time it was necessary to talk naturally. They must still think of me as sitting in the control room.

'That's the ship's generators you're looking at,' I said. 'Ninety-eight per cent of their output is now feeding into coils that make an electromagnet of this ship's hull. You will find it very hard to separate us. And I would advise you not to try.'

The suit was on, and I kept the running chatter up through the mike in the helmet, relaying to the ship's transmitter. The scene in the monitor receiver changed.

'You are now looking at a hydrogen bomb that is primed and aware of the magnetic field holding our ships together. It will, of course, go off if you try to pull away.' I grabbed up the monitor receiver and ran toward the air lock.

'This is a different bomb now,' I said, keeping one eye on the screen and the other on the slowly opening outer door. 'This one has receptors on the hull. If you attempt to destroy any part of this ship, or even gain entry to it, this one will detonate.'

I was in space now, leaping across to the gigantic wall of the other ship.

'What do you want?' These were the first words Pepe had spoken since his first threats.

'I want to talk to you, arrange a deal. Something that would be profitable for both of us. But let me first show you the rest of the bombs, so you won't get any strange ideas about co-operating.'

Of course I *had* to show him the rest of the bombs, there was no getting out of it. The scanners in the ship were following a planned program. I made light talk about all my massive armament that would carry us both to perdition, while I climbed through the hole in the battleship's hull. There was no armor or warning devices at this spot, it had been chosen carefully from the blueprints.

'Yeah, yeah ... I take your word for it, you're a flying bomb. So stop with this roving reporter bit and tell me what you have in mind.'

This time I didn't answer him, because I was running and panting like a dog, and had the mike turned off. Just ahead, if the blueprints were right, was the door to the control room. Pepe should be there.

I stepped through, gun out, and pointed it at the back of his head. Angelina stood next to him, looking at the screen.

'The game's over,' I said. 'Stand up slowly and keep your hands in sight.'

'What do you mean,' he said angrily, looking at the screen in front of him. The girl caught wise first. She spun around and pointed.

'He's *here!*'

They both stared, gaped at me, caught off guard and completely unprepared.

'You're under arrest, crime-king,' I told him. 'And your girl friend.'

Angelina rolled her eyes up and slid slowly to the floor. Real or faked, I didn't care. I kept the gun on Pepe's pudgy form while he picked her up and carried her to an acceleration couch against the wall.

'What … what will happen now?' He quavered the question. His pouchy jaws shook and I swear there were tears in his eyes. I was not impressed by his acting since I could clearly remember the dead men floating in space. He stumbled over to a chair, half dropping into it.

'Will they do anything to me?' Angelina asked. Her eyes were open now.

'I have no idea of what will happen to you.' I told her truthfully. 'That is up to the courts to decide.'

'But he *made* me do all those things,' she wailed. She was young, dark and beautiful, the tears did nothing to spoil this.

Pepe dropped his face into his hands and his shoulders shook. I flicked the gun his way and snapped at him.

'Sit up, Pepe. I find it very hard to believe that you are crying. There are some Naval ships on the way now, the automatic alarm was triggered about a minute ago. I'm sure they'll be glad to see the man who ...'

'Don't let them take me, please!' Angelina was on her feet now, her back pressed to the wall. 'They'll put me in prison, do things to my mind!' She shrank away as she spoke, stumbling along the wall. I looked back at Pepe, not wanting to have my eyes off him for an instant.

'There's nothing I can do,' I told her. I glanced her way and a small door was swinging open and she was gone.

'Don't try to run,' I shouted after her, 'it can't do any good!'

Pepe made a strangling noise and I looked back to him quickly. He was sitting up now and his face was dry of tears. In fact he was laughing, not crying.

'So she caught you, too, Mr Wise-cop, poor little Angelina with the soft eyes.' He broke down again, shaking with laughter.

'What do you mean,' I growled.

'Don't you catch yet? The story she told you was true – except she twisted it around a bit. The whole plan, building the battleship, then stealing it, was *hers*. She pulled me into it, played me like an accordion. I fell in love with her, hating myself and happy at the same time. Well – I'm glad now it's over. At least I gave her a chance to get away, I owe her that much. Though I thought I would explode when she went into that innocence act!'

The cold feeling was now a ball of ice that threatened to paralyze me. 'You're lying,' I said hoarsely, and even I didn't believe it.

'Sorry. That's the way it is. Your brain-boys will

pick my skull to pieces and find out the truth anyway. There's no point in lying now.'

'We'll search the ship, she can't hide for long.'

'She won't have to,' Pepe said. 'There's a fast scout we picked up, stowed in one of the holds. That must be it leaving now.' We could feel the vibration, distantly through the floor.

'The Navy will get her,' I told him, with far more conviction than I felt.

'Maybe,' he said, suddenly slumped and tired, no longer laughing. 'Maybe they will. But I gave her her chance. It is all over for me now, but she knows that I loved her to the end.' He bared his teeth in sudden pain. 'Not that she will care in the slightest.'

I kept the gun on him and neither of us moved while the Navy ships pulled up and their boots stamped outside. I had captured my battleship and the raids were over. And I couldn't be blamed if the girl had slipped away. If she evaded the Navy ships, that was their fault, not mine.

I had my victory all right.

But I wasn't too happy about it. I had a premonition that I wasn't finished with Angelina yet.

CHAPTER

—8—

Life would have been much sweeter if my uneasy hunch hadn't proven to be true. You can't blame the Navy for being taken in by Angelina – they were neither the first nor the last to underestimate the mind that lay behind those melting eyes. And I try not to blame myself either. After my first mistake in letting Angelina slip out I tried not to make a second. I wasn't completely convinced yet that Pepe was telling the truth about her. The entire story might be a complicated lie to confuse and throw me off guard. I have a very suspicious mind. Playing it safe, I kept the muzzle of my gun aimed exactly between his eyes with my fingers resting lightly on the trigger. I kept it there until a squad of space marines thundered in and took over. As soon as they put the grab on Pepe I sent out an all-ships alarm about Angelina, with a special take-all-precautions priority. Even before all the ships had acknowledged receipt her scout rocket was sighted on the detector screen.

I sighed with a great deal of relief. If she did turn out to be the brains of the operation I didn't want her slipping away. She, Pepe and the battleship made a nice package to turn over to Inskipp. There was no chance of her escaping now, with ships closing in on her from every direction. They were experienced at this sort of thing and it was only a matter of time before they had her. Turning over the battleship to the navy, I went back to the luxury yacht and tapped the stores for a large glass of Scotch whisky (that had never been within twenty lightyears of Earth) and a long cigar. Sitting comfortably in front of the screen I monitored the chase.

Angelina wriggled painfully on the hook, making high-G turns to avoid capture. She'd be black and blue from head to foot after some of those 15-G accelerations. It was all for nothing because in the end they still caught her in a tractor web and closed in. All the thrashing around had just gained her a little time. None of us realized how important this time really was until the boarding party cracked into the ship.

It was empty of course.

Fully ten days went by before we pieced together what had really happened. It was ruthless and ugly and even if the psych docs hadn't assured me that Pepe had told the truth, I would have recognized the manner in which the escape was carried out. Angelina was one step ahead of us all the way. When she had escaped from the battleship in the scout rocket she had made no attempt to flee. Instead she must have gone at full blast to the nearest navy ship, a twelve-man pocket cruiser. They of course had no idea what had really happened aboard the battleship, as I hadn't put out the general alarm yet. I should have done that as soon as she had escaped. If I had, twelve good men might still be alive. We'll never know what story she told them, but it was obvious they weren't on their guard.

Probably something about being a prisoner and escaping during the fighting. In any case she took the ship. Five of the men were dead of gas poisoning, the others shot. We discovered this when the cruiser was later found drifting and inert, parsecs away. After capturing the cruiser she had set the controls on the scout ship for evasion tactics and launched it. While we were all merrily chasing it she simply let her ship drop behind the chase and vanished from the fleet. Her trail blurs there, though it is obvious she must have captured another ship. What this ship was, and where she went in it, was a complete mystery.

Back in Corps headquarters, I found myself trying to explain this all to Inskipp. He had a cold eye and hardened manner and I found myself trying to justify my actions.

'You can't win them all,' I said. 'I brought home your battleship and Pepe – may his personality rest in peace now that it has been erased. Angelina tricked me and got away, I'll admit that. But she did a much better job of fooling the boys in the navy!'

'Why so much venom?' Inskipp asked in an arid voice. 'No one's accusing you of dereliction of duty. You sound like a man with a guilty conscience. You did a good job. A fine job. A great job ... for a first assignment. ...'

'You're doing it again!' I howled. 'Prodding my conscience to see how soft it is. Like keeping *him* around.' I pointed to Pepe Nero who was sitting near us in the restaurant eating slowly, mumbling to himself with vacant-eyed dullness. His old personality had been stripped from his mind and a new one implanted. Only the body remained of the old Pepe who had loved Angelina and stolen a battleship.

'The psychs are working on a new theory of body-personality,' Inskipp said blandly, 'so why not keep him around here under observation? If any of his criminal tendencies should develop in the new personality we'll be in a wonderful spot to recruit him for the Corps. Does he bother you?'

'Not him,' I snorted. 'After the massacres he pulled for his psychotic girlfriend you could grind him into hamburger for all I care. But he does remind me that she is still out there somewhere. Free and planning new mischief. I want to go after her.'

'Well you're not,' Inskipp said. 'You've asked me before and I have refused before. The topic is now closed.'

'But I could ...'

'You could *what*?' He gave me a nasty chuckle. 'Every law officer in the galaxy has a pic of her and there is a continual search going on. How could you possibly do more than they are already doing?'

'I couldn't, I guess,' I grumbled. 'So the hell with it, as you say.' I pushed my plate away and stood and stretched as naturally as I could. 'I'm going to get a large jug of liquid refreshment and go to my quarters and nurse my sorrows.'

'You do that. And forget Angelina. Come to my office at 0900 hours tomorrow and you better be sober.'

'Slavedriver,' I moaned, going out to the door and turning down the hall towards the residence wing. As soon as I was out of sight I took a side ramp that led to the spaceport.

That's one lesson I had already learned from Angelina. When you have a plan put it into action instantly. Don't let it lie around and get stale and have

75

other people start thinking about it themselves. I was putting myself up against the shrewdest man in the business now, and the thought alone was enough to make me sweat. I was going against Inskipp's direct orders, walking out on him and the Corps. Not really walking out, since I only wanted to finish the job I had started for them. But I was obviously the only one who would look at it that way.

There were tools, gadgets and a good deal of money in my quarters that would come in very handy on this job. I would just have to do without them. When Inskipp started to think about my sudden conversion to his point of view I wanted to be well away in space.

A mechanic with a drag-robot was pulling an agent's ship into place on the launching ramp. I stamped over and used my official voice.

'Is that my ship?'

'No, sir – it's for Full Agent Nielson, there he is coming up now.'

'Check with central control, will you? It's going to be rush no matter how we handle it.'

'New job, Jimmy?' Ove asked as he came up. I nodded and watched the mechanic until he vanished around the corner.

'Same old business,' I said. 'And how's your tennis game coming?' I asked, lifting my hand with an imaginary racket.

'Getting better all the time,' he said, turning his head to look at his ship.

'I'll teach you a new stroke,' I said, bringing my hand down sharply and catching him on the side of the neck with the straightened edge. He folded without a sound and I lowered him gently to the deck and dragged him out of sight behind a row of lubrication drums. I gently pried the box with the course tapes from his limp fingers.

Before the mechanic could return I was in the ship and had the lock sealed. I fed the course tape into the controls and punched the tower combination for clearance. There was a subjective century of waiting, during which eternal period of time I produced a fine beading of sweat all over my head. Then the green light came on.

Step one and still in the clear. As soon as the launching acceleration stopped I was out of the chair and attacking the control panel with the screwdriver ready in my hand. There was always a remote control unit here so that any Corps ship could be flown from a distance. I had discovered it on my first flight in one of these ships since I have always maintained that there is a positive value to being nosey. I disconnected the input and output leads, then dived for the engine room.

Perhaps I am too suspicious or have too low an opinion of mankind. Or of Inskipp, who had his own rules on most subjects. Someone more trusting than I would have ignored the radio controlled suicide bomb built into the engine. This could be used to scuttle the ship in case of capture. I didn't think they would use it on me except as a last resort. Nevertheless I still wanted it disconnected.

The bomb was an integral part of the engine mounting, a solid block of burmedex built into the casing. The lid dropped off easily enough and inside there was a maze of circuits all leading to a fuse screwed into the thick metal. It had a big hex-head on it and I scraped my knuckles trying to get a wrench around it and turn it in the close quarters. With a last grate of bruised flesh and knuckle bones I twisted it free. It hung down from its wire leads, a nerve drawn from a deadly tooth.

Then it exploded with a loud bang and a cloud of black smoke.

With most unnatural calm I looked from the cloud of dispersing smoke back to the black hole in the bermedex charge. This would have turned the ship and its contents into a fine dust.

'Inskipp,' I said, but my throat was dry and my voice cracked and I had to start again. 'Inskipp, I get your message. You thought you were giving me my discharge. Accept instead my resignation from the Special Corps.'

CHAPTER

— 9 —

My most overwhelming feeling was one of relief. I was on my own again and responsible to no man. I actually hummed a bit as I dropped the ship out of warpdrive long enough to slip in a course tape chosen at random from the file. There would be no chance of an intercept this way and I could cut a tape for a new course once I was well clear of the headquarters station.

A course to where? I wasn't sure yet. That would require a bit of research, though there was no doubt about what I would be doing. Looking for Angelina. At first thought it seemed a little stupid to be taking on a job the Corps had refused me. It was still their job. On second thought I realized that it had nothing to do with the Corps now. Angy had pulled a fast one on me, pinned on the prize-chump medal. That is something that you just don't do to Slippery Jim diGriz. Call it ego if you like. But ego is the only thing that keeps a man in my profession operating. Remove that and you have removed everything. I had no real idea of what I would do with her when I found her. Probably turn her over to the police, since people like her gave the business a bad name. Better to worry about cooking the fish after I had caught it.

A plan was necessary, so I prepared all the plan producing ingredients. For one terrible moment I thought there were no cigars in the ship. Then the service unit groaned and produced a box from some dark corner of the deep freeze. Not the recommended way to store cigars, but much better than having none at all. Nielsen always favored a rare brand of potent akvavit and I had no objections to drinking it. Feet up, throat lubricated and cigar smoking, I put the think-box to work on the project.

To begin with, I had to put myself in Angelina's place at the time of her escape. I would like to have gone back physically to the scene, but I'm not that thick. There was guaranteed to be a trigger-happy navy ship or two sitting there. However this is the kind of problem they build computers to solve, so I fed in the coordinates of the space action where it all had happened. There was no need for notes on this – those figures were scratched inside my forehead in letters of fire. The computer had a large memory store and a high speed scan. It hummed happily when I asked for the stars nearest to the given position. In under thirteen seconds it flipped through its catalogs, counted on its fingers and rang its little computation-finished bell for me. I copied off the numbers of the first dozens stars, then pressed the cancel when I saw the distances were getting too great to be relevant anymore.

Now I must think like Angelina. I had to be hunted, hurried, a murderess with twelve fresh corpses of my own manufacture piled around me. In every direction rode the enemy. She would have the same list, ground out by the computer on the stolen cruiser. Now – where to? Tension and speed. Get going somewhere. Somewhere away from here. A glance at the list and the answer seemed obvious. The two nearest stars were in the same quadrant of the sky, within fifteen degrees of each other. They were roughly equidistant. What was more important was the fact that star number three was in a different sector of the sky and twice as far away.

That was the way to go, toward the first two stars. It was the sort of decision that can be made in a hurry and still be sound. Head toward suns and worlds and the lanes where other ships could be found. The cruiser would have to be gotten rid of before any planets were approached – the faster the better since every ship in the galaxy would be looking for it. Then meet another ship – ship X – and capture it. Abandon the cruiser and … do what?

My tenuous line of logic was ready to snap at this point so I strengthened it with some akvavit and a fresh cigar. With my eyes half closed in reverie I tried to rebuild the flight. Capture the new ship and – head for a planet. As long as she was alone in space Angelina was in constant danger. A planetfall and a change of personality were called for. When I looked up those two target stars in the catalog the planetary choice was obvious. A barbaric sounding place named Freibur.

There were a half dozen other settled planets around the two suns, but all eliminated themselves easily. Either too lightly settled, so that a stranger would be easily spotted, or organized and integrated so well that it would be impossible to be around long without some notice being taken. Freibur shared none of these difficulties. It had been in the league for less than two hundred years, and would be in a happily chaotic state. A mixture of the old and new, pre-contact culture and post-contact civilization. The perfect place for her to slip into quietly, and lose herself until she could appear with a fresh identity.

Reaching this conclusion produced a double glow of satisfaction. This was more than a mental exercise in survival since I was now roughly in the same place Angelina had been. The incident with the scuttling charge was a strong indication of the value the Corps put on their ships – and the low value they placed on deserters. Freibur was a place that would suit me perfectly. I retired happily with a slight buzz on and a scorched mouth from the dehydrated cigars.

When I dragged myself back to consciousness it was time to drop out of warpspace and plot a new course. Except there was one thing I had to do first. A lot of the little facts I knew had *not* been picked up in the Corps. One fact – normally of interest only to warpdrive technicians – concerns the curious propagation of radiation in warpspace. Radio waves in particular. They just don't go anyplace. If you broadcast on one frequency you get a strong return signal on all frequencies, as if the radio waves had been squeezed out thin and bounced right back. Normally of no interest, this exotic phenomena is just the thing to find out if your ship is bugged. I put nothing beyond the Special Corps, and bugging their own ships seemed a logical precaution. A concealed radio, transmitting on a narrow band, would lead them right to me wherever I went. This I had to find out before getting near any planets.

There was a squeal and a growl from the speaker and I cursed my former employers. But before I wasted my time looking for a transmitter I ought to be sure one was there. Whatever was producing the signal seemed too weak to be picked up at any distance. Some quick work with a few sheets of shielding showed that my mysterious signal was nothing more than leaking radiation from the receiver itself. After it was shielded the ether was quiet. I enjoyed a sigh of justified satisfaction and dropped out of warp.

Once I had a course plotted the trip wasn't a long one. I took the opportunity to scrounge through the ship's equipment and put together a kit for future use. The elaborate make-up and appearance-alteration machinery begged to be used, and of course I did. Rebuilding the working-personality of Slippery Jim was a positive pleasure. As the nose plugs and cheek pads skipped into place and the dye seeped into my hair I sighed and relaxed with happiness, an old war horse getting back on the job.

Then I scowled, growled at myself in the mirror and began to remove the disguise as carefully as I had assumed it. It has always been anxiomatic with me that there is no relaxation in this line of business, and anything done by rote usually leads to disaster. Inskipp knew my old working personality only too well and they would surely be looking for me under that description as well as my normal one. The second time around I took a little more care with the disguise and built up an entirely different appearance. A simple one – with facial and hair changes – that would be easily maintained. The more elaborate a job of make-up is the more time it takes to keep it accurate. Freibur was a big question-mark so far and I didn't want to be loaded with any extra responsibilities like this. I wanted to go in relaxed, sniff around and see if I could pick up Angelina's trail.

There were still two subjective days left in warpdrive

and I put these to good use making some simple gadgetry that might come in handy. Pinhead grenades, tie-clasp pistols, ring-drills – the usual thing. I only brushed away the scraps and cleaned the shop up when the ship signaled the end of the trip.

The only city on Freibur with a ground controlled spaceport was at Freiburbad, which was situated on the shore of an immense lake, the only sizeable body of fresh water on the planet. Looking at the sunlight glinting from it I had the sudden desire for a swim. This urge must have been the genesis of my idea to drown the stolen ship. Leave it at the bottom of a deep spot in the lake and it would always be handy if needed.

I made planetfall over a jagged mountain range and picked up not as much as a beep on the radar. Coming in over the lake after dark I detected navigation radar from the spaceport, but my ship wouldn't get too far inshore. A rainstorm – cut through with hail – shortened visibility and removed my earlier bathing desire. There was a deep underwater channel not too far from the shore and I touched down above it while I put my kit together. It would be foolish to carry too much, but some of the Corps gear was too valuable to leave behind. Sealing it in a waterproof cover I strapped it to my spacesuit and opened the air lock. Rain and darkness washed over me as I struck out for the unseen shore. I imagined rather than heard the gurgle behind me as the ship sank gently to the bottom.

Swimming in a spacesuit is about as easy to manage as making love in free fall. I churned my way to shore in a state of near exhaustion. After crawling out of the suit I had a great deal of pleasure watching it burn to a cinder under the heat of three thermite bombs. I particularly enjoyed kicking the resultant hissing slag into the lake. The rain hammered down and washed all traces of the burning away. Apparently even the fierce light of the thermite had gone unobserved in the downpour. Huddling under a waterproof sheet I waited damply and miserably for dawn.

Sometime during the night I dozed off without meaning to because it was already light when I woke up. Something was very wrong, and before I could remember what had woken me the voice called again.

'Going to Freiburbad? Of course, where else is there to go? I'm going there myself. Got a boat. Old boat but a good boat. Beats walking ...'

The voice went on and on, but I wasn't listening. I was cursing myself for being caught unaware by this joker with the long-playing voice. He was riding in a small boat just off shore; the thing was low in the water with bales and bundles, and the man's head stuck above the top of everything. While his jaw kept moving I had a chance to look at him and draw my sleep-sodden wits together. He had a wild and bristly beard that stuck out in all directions, and tiny dark eyes hidden under the most decrepit hat I had ever seen. Some of my startled panic ebbed away. If this oddball wasn't a plant, the accidental meeting might be turned to my benefit.

When mattress-face stopped to drag in a long overdue breath I accepted his offer and reached for the gunwale of the boat and drew it closer. I picked up my bundle – getting my hand on my gunbutt as I did it – and jumped in. There didn't seem to be any need for caution. Zug – that was his name, I plucked it out of the flowing stream of his monologue – bent over an outboard motor clamped to the stern and coaxed it to life. It was a tired looking atomic heat-exchanger, simple but efficient. No moving parts, it simply sucked in cold lake water, heated it to a boil and shot it out through an underwater jet. Made almost no sound while running, which was how the rig had slid up without wakening me.

Everything about Zug seemed normal – I still wasn't completely convinced and kept the gun close to my hand – but if it was normal I had hit a piece of luck. His cataract of words washed over me and I began to understand why. Apparently he was a hunter, bringing his pelts to market after months of solitude and silence. The sight of a human face had induced a sort of verbal diarrhea which I made no attempt to stop. He was answering a lot of questions for me.

One thing that had been a worry were my clothes. I had finally decided to wear a one-piece ship suit, done in neutral gray. You see this kind of outfit, with minor variations, on planets right across the galaxy. It had passed unnoticed by Zug, which wasn't really saying much since he was anything but a clothes fancier. He must have made his jacket himself out of the local fur. It was purplish-black and must have been very fine before the grease and twigs had been rubbed in. His pants were made of machine-woven cloth and his boots were the same as mine, of eternene plastic. If he was allowed to walk around loose in this outfit, mine would surely never be noticed.

What I could see of Zug's equipment bore out the impression gained from his clothes. The old and new mixed together. A world like Freibur, not too long in the League, would be expected to be like that. The electrostatic rifle leaning against a bundle of steel bolts for the crossbow made a typical picture. Undoubtedly the Voice of The Wilderness here could use both weapons with equal facility. I settled down on the soft bundles and enjoyed the voyage and the visual pleasures of the misty dawn, bathed continually in a flow of words.

We reached Freiburbad before noon. Zug had more of an ambition to talk than to be talked to, and a few vague remarks of mine about going to the city satisfied him. He greatly enjoyed the food concentrates from my pack and reciprocated by producing a flask of some noxious home brew he had distilled in his mountain retreat. The taste was indescribably awful and left the mouth feeling as if it had been rasped by steel wool soaked in sulphuric acid. But the first few drinks numbed and after that we enjoyed the trip – until we tied up at a fish-smelling dock outside the city. We almost swamped the boat getting out of it, which we thought hysterically funny, and which will give you some indication of our mental state at the time. I walked into the city proper and sat in a park until my head cleared.

The old and the new pressed shoulders here, plastic fronted buildings wedged in between brick and plaster. Steel, glass, wood and stone all mixed with complete indifference. The people were the same, dressed in a strange mixture of types and styles. I took more notice of them than they did of me. A newsrobot was the only thing that singled me out for attention. It blatted its dull offerings in my ear and waved a board with the printed headlines until I bought a paper to get rid of it. League currency was in circulation here, as well as local money, and the robot made no protest when I slipped a credit in its chest slot, though it did give me change in Freibur *gilden* – undoubtedly at a ruinous rate of exchange. At least that's the way I would have done it if I were programming the thing.

All of the news was unimportant and trivial – the advertisements were of much more interest. Looking through the big hotels I compared their offered pleasures and prices.

It was this that set me to trembling and sweating with terror. How quickly we lose the ingrained habits of a lifetime. After a month on the side of law and order I was acting like an honest man!

'You're a criminal,' I muttered through clenched teeth, and spat on a NO SPITTING sign. 'You hate the law and live happily without it. You are a law unto yourself, and the most honest man in the galaxy. You can't break any rules since you make them up yourself and change them whenever you see fit.'

All of this was true, and I hated myself for forgetting it. That little period of honesty in the Corps was working like a blight to destroy all of my best anti-social tendencies.

'Think dirty!' I cried aloud, startling a girl who was walking by on the path. I leered to prove that she had heard correctly and she hurried quickly away. That was better. I left myself at the same time, in the opposite direction, looking for an opportunity to do bad. I had to reestablish my identity before I could even consider finding Angelina.

Opportunity was easy to find. Within ten minutes I had spotted my target. I had all the equipment I might need in my sack. What I would use for the job I stowed in my pockets and waist wallet, then checked my bag in a public locker.

Everything about the First Bank of Freibur begged to

be cracked. It had three entrances, four guards and was busily crowded. Four human guards! No bank in existence would pay all those salaries if they had electronic protection. It was an effort not to hum with happiness as I stood in line for one of the *human* clerks. Fully automated banks aren't hard to rob, they just require different techniques. This mixture of man and machine was the easiest of all.

'Change a League ten-star for gilden,' I said, slapping the shiny coin on the counter before him.

'Yessir,' the cashier said, only glancing at the coin and feeding it into the accounting machine next to him. His fingers had already set up the amount for me in gilden, even before the *currency valid* signal blinked on. My money rattled down into the cup before me and I counted it slowly. This was done mechanically, because my mind was really on the ten credit coin now rolling and clinking down inside the machine's innards. When I was sure it had finished its trip and landed in the vault I pressed the button on my wrist transmitter.

It was beautiful, that was the only word for it. The kind of thing that leaves a warm glow lodged in the memory, that produces a twinge of happiness for years after whenever it is nudged. That little ten credit coin had taken hours to construct and every minute was worth it. I had sliced it in half, hollowed it out, loaded it with lead back to its original weight, built in a tiny radio receiver, a fuse and a charge of burmedex, which now went off with an incredibly satisfactory explosion. A grinding thump deep in the bank's entrails was followed by a tremendous amount of clanking and banging. The rear wall – containing the vault – split open and disgorged a torrent of money and smoke.

Some last effort of the expiring accounting machine gave me an unexpected dividend. The money dispensers at every cashier's station burst into frantic life. A torrent of large and small coins poured out on the startled customers who quickly mastered their surprise and began grabbing. Their moment of pleasure was brief because the same radio cue had set off the smoke and gas bombs I had thoughtfully dropped in all the wastebaskets. Unnoticed in the excitement, I threw a few more gas bombs in with the cashiers. This gas is an effective mixture of my own concoction, a sinister brew of regurgitants and lachrymatories. Its effect was instantaneous and powerful. (There were of course no children in the bank, since I don't believe in being cruel to those too young to protect themselves.) Within seconds the clients and employees found themselves unable to see, and too preoccupied to take any notice of me.

As the gas rolled towards me I lowered my head and slipped the goggles over my eyes. When I looked up I was the only person in the bank that was able to see. I was of course careful to breathe through the filter plugs in my nose, so I could enjoy the continued digestion of my last meal. My teller had vanished from sight and I did a neat dive through the opening, sliding across the counter on my stomach.

After this it was just a matter of pick and choose, there was certainly no shortage of money rolling around loose. I ignored the small stuff and went to the source, the riven vault out of which poured a golden torrent. Within two minutes I had filled the bag I had brought and was ready to leave. The smoke near the doors was thinning a bit, but a few more grenades took care of that.

Everything was working perfectly and under control, except for one fool of a guard who was making a nuisance of himself. His tiny brain realized dimly that something wrong was going on, so he was staggering in circles firing his gun. It was a wonder he hadn't hit anyone yet. I took the gun away and hit him on the head with it.

The smoke was densest near the doors, making it impossible to see out. It was just as impossible of course to see in, so no one in the street had any real idea of what had happened. They of course knew *something* was wrong; two policemen had rushed in with guns drawn ... but were now as helpless as the rest. I organized the relief of the sufferers then, and began pulling and guiding them to the door. When I had enough of a crowd collected I joined them and we all crawled out into the street together. I put the goggles in my pocket and kept my eyes closed until I had groped clear of the gas. Some worthy citizens helped me and I thanked them, tears streaming down my face from the fringes of the gas, and went my way.

That's how easy it is. That's how easy it always is if you plan ahead and don't take foolish risks. My morale was high and the blood sang in my veins. Life was deliciously crooked and worth living again. Finding Angelina's trail now would be simplicity itself. There was nothing I couldn't do.

Staying on the crest of this emotional wave, I rented a room in a spacemen's hotel near the port, cleaned up and strode forth to enjoy the pleasures of life. There were many rough-and-ready joints in the area and I made the rounds. I had a steak in one and a drink apiece in each of the others. If Angelina had come to Freibur she would surely have passed – at least briefly –

through this area. The trail would be here, I felt that in my bones. Crooked bones once again, and sympathetic to her own lawlessness.

'Howsabout buying a girl a drink,' the tart said spiritlessly, and I shook my head no with the same lack of interest. The hostesses, pallid creatures of the night, were coming out as the evening progressed. I was getting a good share of propositions since I had taken care to look like a spaceman on leave, always a good source of revenue for these women. This one was the latest of a number who had approached me. A little better looking than most, at least better constructed. I watched her walking away with interest that bordered on admiration. Her skirt was short, tight and slashed high up on the sides. High heels lent a rotating motion to this, producing a most effective result. She reached the bar and turned to survey the room, and I couldn't help but appreciate the rest of her. Her blouse was made of thin strips of shimmering fabric, joined together only at the tops and bottoms. They separated to reveal enticing slices of creamy skin whenever she moved, and I'm sure had the desired effect on masculine libidos.

My eyes finally reached her face – a long trip since I had started the survey at her ankles – and she was quite attractive. Almost familiar ...

Exactly at this instant my heart gave a grinding thud in my chest and I grew rigid in my chair. It seemed impossible – yet it had to be true.

She was Angelina.

CHAPTER

-10-

Her hair had been bleached and there were some simple and obvious changes in her features. They had been altered just enough so it would be impossible to identify her from a photograph or a description. She could never be recognized.

Except by me, that is. I had seen her in the stolen battleship and I had talked to her. And the nice part was I could identify her and she would have no idea of who I was. She had seen me only briefly – in a spacesuit with a tinted faceplate – and I'm sure had plenty of other things to think about at the time.

This was the climax of the most successful day of my life. The fetid air of the dive was like wine in my nostrils. I relaxed and savored every last drop of irony in the situation. You had to give the girl credit, though. She had adopted a perfect cover. I myself had never imagined she would stay here, and I thought I had weighed all of the possibilities. Because she had taken a good bit of the stolen cash with her, I had never considered she would be living like a penniless tramp. The girl had guts, you had to give her credit. She had adopted an almost perfect disguise and blended neatly into the background. If only she wasn't so damned kill-happy – what a team we would make!

My heart gave the second grinding thump of the evening when I realized the dead-end trail down which my emotions were leading me. Angelina was disaster to anyone she came near. Inside that lovely head squatted a highly intelligent but strangely warped brain. For my own sake I would be better off thinking about the corpses she had piled up, not about her figure. There was only one thing to be done. Get her away from here and turn her over to the Corps. I didn't even consider how I felt about the Corps – or how they felt about me. This was an entirely different affair that had to be done neatly and with dispatch before I changed my mind.

I joined her at the bar and ordered two double shots of the local battery acid. Being careful, I deepened my voice and changed my accent and manner of speaking. Angelina had heard enough of my voice to identify it easily – that was the one thing I had to be aware of.

'Drink up, doll,' I said, raising my drink and leering at her. 'Then we go up to your place. You got a place don't you?'

'I gotta place you gotta League ten-spot in hard change?'

'Of course,' I grumbled, feigning insult. 'You think I'm buying this bilge-juice on the arm?'

'I ain't no cafeteria pay-on-your-way-out,' she said with a bored lack of interest that was magnificent. 'Pay now and then we go.'

When I flipped the ten credits her way she speared it neatly out of the air, weighed it, bit it, and vanished it inside her belt. I looked on with frank admiration, which she would mistake for carnal interest, but was in reality appreciation of the faultless manner with which she played her role. Only when she turned away did I make myself remember that this was business not pleasure, and I had a stern duty to perform. My resolution was wavering and I screwed it tight again with a memory of corpses floating in space. Draining my glass I followed her marvelous rotation out of the bar and down a noisome alley.

The dark decrepitude of the narrow passage jarred my reflexes awake. Angelina played her part well, but I doubted if she bedded down with all the space tramps who hit this port. There was a good chance that she had a confederate around who had a strong right arm with a heavy object clutched tightly in his hand. Or perhaps I'm naturally suspicious. My hand was on the gun in my pocket but I didn't need to use it. We treaded across another street and turned into a hallway. She went first and we didn't talk. No one came near us or even bothered to notice us. When she unlocked her room I relaxed a bit. It was small and tawdry, but offered no possible hiding place for an accomplice. Angelina went straight to the bed and I checked the door to see if it really was locked. It was.

When I turned around she was pointing a .75 caliber recoilless automatic at me, so big and ugly that she had to hold it in both tiny hands.

'What the hell is the racket?' I blustered, fighting back the sick sensation that I had missed an important clue someplace along the line. My hand was still on the gun in my pocket but trying to draw it would be instant suicide.

'I'm going to kill you without ever even knowing your name,' she said sweetly, with a cute smile that showed even white teeth. 'But you have this coming for ruining my battleship operation.'

Still she didn't fire, but her grin widened until it was almost a laugh. She was enjoying the uncontrolled expressions on my face as I recognized the fact that I had been out-thought all the way along the line. That the trapper was the trappee. That she had me exactly precisely where she wanted me and there wasn't a single bloody damn thing I could do about it.

Angelina finally had to laugh out loud, a laugh clear and charming as a silver bell, as she watched me reach these sickening conclusions one after another. She was an artist to her fingertips and waited just long enough for me to understand everything. Then, at the exact and ultimate moment of my maximum realization and despair, she pulled the trigger.

Not once, but over and over again.

Four tearing, thundering bullets of pain directly into my heart. And a final slug directly between my eyes.

CHAPTER
–11–

It wasn't really consciousness, but a sort of ruddy, pain-filled blur. A gut-gripping nausea fought with the pain, but won easily. Part of the trouble was that my eyes were closed, yet opening them was incredibly difficult. I finally managed it and could make out a face swimming in a blur above me.

'What happened?' the blur asked.

'I was going to ask you the same thing . . .' I said, and stopped, surprised at how weak and bubbly my voice was. Something brushed across my lips and I saw a red-stained pad as it went away.

After I blinked some sight back into my eyes, blur-face turned out to be a youngish man dressed in white. A doctor, I suppose, and I was aware of motion; we must be driving in an ambulance.

'Who shot you?' the doctor asked. 'Someone reported the shots and you'll be pleased to know we got there just in the old nick of time. You've lost a lot of blood – some of which I've replaced – have multiple fractures of the radius and ulna, an extensive bullet wound in your forearm, a further wound in your right temple, possible fracture of the skull, extremely probable fractures in your ribs and the possibility of internal injuries. Someone got a grudge against you? Who?'

Who? My darling Angelina, that's who. Temptress, sorceress, murderess, that's who tried to kill me. I remembered now. The wide black muzzle of the gun looking big enough to park a spaceship in. The fire blasting out of it, the slugs hammering into me, and the pain as my expensive, guaranteed, bulletproof underwear soaked up the impact of the bullets, spreading it across the entire front of my body. I remembered the hope that this would satisfy her and the despair of hope as the muzzle of that reeking gun lifted to my face.

I remembered the last instant of regret as I put my arms before my face and threw myself sideways in a vain attempt at escape.

The funny thing is that escape attempt had worked. The bullet that had smashed my forearm must have been deflected enough by the bone to carom off my skull, instead of catching it point blank and drilling on through. All this had produced satisfactory quantities of blood and an immobile body on the floor. That had caused Angelina's mistake, her only one. The boom of the gun in that tiny room, my apparent corpse, the blood, it must have all rattled the female side of her, at least a bit. She had to leave fast before the shots were investigated and she had not taken that extra bit of time to make sure.

'Lie down,' the doctor said. 'I'll give you an injection that will knock you out for a week if you don't lie down!'

Only when he said this did I realize I was half sitting up in the stretcher and chuckling a particularly dirty laugh. I let myself be pushed down easily, since my chest was drenched in pain whenever I moved.

Right at that moment my mind began ticking over plans for making the most of the situation. Ignoring the pain as well as I could, I looked around the ambulance, looking for a way to capitalize on the bit of luck that had kept me still alive while she thought I was dead.

We pulled up at the hospital then, and there was nothing much I could do in the ambulance except steal the stylus and official forms from the rack above my head. My right arm was still good, though it hurt like fire whenever I moved. A robot snapped the wheels down on my stretcher, latched onto it and wheeled it inside. As it went by the doctor he slipped some papers into a holder near my head and waved good-by to me. I gave him back a gallant smile as I turned into the butcher shop.

As soon as he was out of sight I pulled out the papers and scanned them quickly. Here lay my opportunity if I had enough time to grab it. There was the doctor's report – in quadruplicate. Until these forms were fed into the machinery I didn't exist. I was in a statistical limbo out of which I would be born into the hospital. Stillborn if I had my way. I pushed my pillow off onto the corridor floor and the robot stopped. He paid no attention to my writing and didn't seem to mind stopping two more times to rescue the pillow, giving me time to finish my forgery.

This Doctor Mcvbklz – at least that's what his signature reads like – had a lot to learn about signing papers. He had left acres of clear space between the last line of the report and his signature. I filled this with a very passable imitation of his handwriting.

Massive internal hemorrhage, shock ... I wrote, *died en route.* This sounded official enough. I quickly added *All attempts resuscitation failed.* I had a moment of doubt about spelling this jaw breaker, but since Dr Mcvbklz thought there were two P's in *multiple* he could be expected to muff this one too. This last line made sure there wouldn't be any hanky-panky with needles and electric prods to jazz some life back into the corpse. We turned out of the corridor just as I slipped the forms back into their slot and lay back trying to look dead.

'Here's a D.O.A., Svend,' someone called out, rustling the papers behind my head. I heard the robot rolling away, untroubled by the fact that his writing, pillow-shedding patient was suddenly dead. This lack of curiosity is what I like about robots. I tried to think dead thoughts and hoped the right expression was showing on my face. Something jerked at my left foot and my boot and sock were pulled off. A hand grabbed my foot.

'How tragic,' this sympathetic soul said, 'he's still warm. Maybe we should put him on the table and get the revival team down.' What a nosy, mealy-mouthed, interfering sod he was.

'Nah,' the voice of a wiser and cooler head said from across the room. 'They tried the works in the ambulance. Slide him in the box.'

A terrifying pain lanced through my foot and I almost gave the whole show away. Only the fiercest control enabled me to lie unmoving while this clown grimly tightened the wire around my big toe. There was a tag hanging from the wire and I heartily wished the same tag was hung from his ear secured by the same throttling wire. Pain from the toe washed up and joined the ache in my chest, head and arm, and I fought for corpselike rigidity as the stretcher trundled along.

Somewhere behind me a heavy door opened and a wave of frigid air struck my skin. I allowed myself a quick look through my lashes. If the corpses in this chop shop were stashed into individual freezers I was about to be suddenly restored to life. I could think of a lot more pleasant ways of dying than in an ice box with the door handle on the outside. Lady Luck was still galloping along at my shoulder because my toe-amputator was dragging me, stretcher and all, into a good-sized room. There were slabs on all sides and a number of dearly departed had already arrived before me.

With no attempt at gentleness I was slid onto a freezing surface. Footsteps went away from me across the room, the door closed heavily and the lights went out.

My morale hit bottom at this moment. I had been through a lot for one day, and was thoroughly battered, bruised, contused and concussed. Being locked in a black room full of corpses had an unusually depressing effect on me. In spite of the pain in my chest and the tag trailing from my toe, I managed to slide off the slab and hobble to the door. Panic grew as I lost my direction, easing off only when I walked square into the wall. My fingers found a switch and the lights came back on. And of course my moral fiber stiffened at the same moment.

The door was perfectly designed, I couldn't have done better myself, with no window and a handle on the inside. There was even a bolt so that it could be locked from this side, though for what hideous reason

I couldn't possibly imagine. It gave me some needed privacy though, so I slipped it into place.

Although the room was full, no one was paying any attention to me. The first thing I did was unwind the wire and massage some life back into my numb toe. On the yellow tag were the large black letters D.O.A. and a handwritten number, the same one that had been on the form I had altered. This was too good an opportunity to miss. I took the tag off the toe of the most badly battered male corpse and substituted mine. His tag I pocketed, then spent a merry few minutes changing around all the other tags. During this process I took a right shoe from the corpse with the biggest feet and jammed my frozen left foot into it. All the tags were hung from the left big toe and I loudly cursed such needless precision. My chest was bare where my shipsuit and bulletproof cover had been cut away. One of my silent friends had a warm shirt he didn't need, so I borrowed that too.

Don't think for a second that all this was easy. I was staggering and mumbling to myself while I did it. When it was finished I slapped off the light and cracked the door of the freezer. The air from the hall felt like a furnace. There wasn't a soul in sight so I closed the vault and staggered over to the nearest door. It was to a storeroom and the only thing there that I could use was a chair. I sat in this as long as I dared, then went looking again. The next door was locked but the third one opened to a dark room where I could hear someone breathing evenly in his sleep. This was more like it.

Whoever this sacktime artist was, he surely knew his sleeping trade. I rifled the room and fumbled with the clothes I found and put them on clumsily – yet he never heard a sound. Which was probably the best thing for him because I was in a skull-fracturing humor. The novelty of this little affair had worn off and all I could think about was the pain. There was a hat too, so I put this on and checked out. I saw people at a distance, but no one was watching when I pushed open an emergency exit and found myself back on the rain-drenched streets of Freiburbad.

CHAPTER

– 12 –

That night and the next few days are hazy in the memory for obvious reasons. It was a risk to go back to my room, but a calculated one. The chances were good that Angelina didn't know of its existence or, even if she had found out, that she wouldn't have done anything about it. I was dead and she had no further interest in me. This appeared to be true, because I wasn't bothered after I was in the room. I had the management send up some food and at least two bottles of liquor a day so it would look like I was on an extended and solitary bender. The rotgut went down the drain and I picked a bit at the food while my body slowly recovered. I kept my aching flesh drenched in antibiotics and loaded with pain-killers, and counted myself lucky.

On the third morning I felt weak but almost human. My arm in the cast throbbed when I moved it, the black and blue marks on my chest were turning gorgeous shades of violet and gold, but my headache was almost gone. It was time to plan for the future. I sipped some of the liquor I had been using to flush out the plumbing and called down for the newspapers of the past three days. The ancient delivery tube wheezed and disgorged them onto the table. Going through them carefully, I was pleased to discover that my plan had worked much better than should have been expected.

The day after my murder there had been items in every paper about it, grubbed from the hospital records by the slothful newshounds who hadn't even bothered to glance at the corpse. That was all. Nothing later about Big Hospital Scandal in Missing Corpse or Suit Brought Because That's Not Uncle Frim In The Coffin. If my jiggery-pokery in the frozen meat locker had been uncovered, it was being kept a hospital family secret and heads were rolling in private.

Angelina, my sharpshooting sweetheart, must then think of me as securely dead, a victim of her own murderous trigger finger. Nothing could be better. As soon as I was able to I would be getting back on her trail again, the job of tracking her made immensely simpler by her believing me to be a wisp of greasy smoke in the local crematorium. There was plenty of time now to plan this thing and plan it right. No more funny business about who was hunting whom. I was going to get as much pleasure out of arresting Angelina as she had derived from blasting away at me with her portable artillery.

It was a humiliating but true fact that she had outmaneuvered me all the way down the line. She had stolen the battleship from under my nose, torn a wide swath through galactic shipping, then escaped neatly right under my gun. What made the situation most embarrassing was that she had set a trap for me – when I thought I was hunting her. Hindsight is a great revealer of obviousities and this one was painfully clear now. While escaping from the captured battle-ship she had not been hysterical in the slightest. That role had been feigned. She had been studying me, every bit of my face that could be seen, every intonation of my voice. Hatred had seared my picture in her memory, and while escaping she must have considered constantly how I would be thinking when I followed her. At the safest and least obvious spot in her flight she had stopped – and waited. Knowing I would come and knowing that she would be more prepared for the encounter than I was. This was all past history. Now it was my turn to deal the cards.

All kinds of schemes and plans trotted through my head to be weighed and sampled. Top priority – before anything else was attempted – would be a complete physical change for me. This would be necessary if I wanted to catch up with Angelina. It was also required if I were to stay out of the long reach of the Corps. The fact had not been mentioned during my training, but I was fairly sure the only way one left the Special Corps was feet first. Though I was physically down and out there was nothing wrong with the old think box and I put it to use. Facts were needed, and I gave a small endowment to the city library in the form of rental fees. Fortunately there were filmcopies of all the local newspapers available, going back for years. I made the acquaintance of an extremely yellowish journal endearingly called 'HOT NEWS!!' *Hot News!!* aimed at a popular readership – with a vocabulary I estimated at approximately three hundred words – who relished violence in its multiform aspects. Most of the time these were just copter accidents and such, with full color photos of course. But very often there were juicy muggings, sluggings and such which proved the quieting hand of galactic civilization still hadn't throttled Freibur completely. In among these exaggerated tales of violence lay the murky crime I was searching for.

Mankind has always been capricious in it lawmaking, inventing such intriguingly different terms as manslaughter, justified homicide and such, as if dead wasn't dead. Though fashions in both crime and sentencing come and go, there is one crime that will always bring universal detestation. That is the crime of being a bungling doctor. I have heard tell that certain savage tribes used to slaughter the physician if his patient died, a system that is not without merit. This singleminded loathing of the butchering quack is understandable. When ill, we deliver ourselves completely into the doctor's hands. We give a complete stranger the opportunity to toy with that which we value most. If this trust is violated there is naturally a hotness of temper among the witness or survivors.

Ordinary-citizen Vulff Sifternitz had formerly been the Highly Esteemed Doctor Sifternitz. *Hot News!!* explained in overly lavish detail how he had mixed the life of Playboy and Surgeon until finally the knife in his twitching fingers had cut *that* instead of *this* and the life of a prominent politician had been shortened by a number of no doubt profitable years. We must give Vulff credit for the fact that he had made an attempt to sober up before going to work, so that it was D.T.'s, not drunkenness, that caused the fatal twitch. His license was removed and he must have been fined most of his savings since there were later references to his having been involved in more sordid medical affairs. Life had treated Vulff hard and dirty; he was just the man I was looking for. On my first rubber-legged trip out of my room I took the liberty of paying him a professional call.

To a person of my abilities tracking down a pseudo-legal stranger in a foreign city on a far planet presents no problems. Just a matter of technique and I am rich in technique. When I hammered on the stained wooden door in the least-wholesome section of town I was ready to take the first step in my new plan.

'I have some business for you, Vulff,' I told the bleary-eyed stewie who opened the door.

'Get the hell lost,' he said and tried to close the door in my face. My carefully placed shoe prevented this and it took almost no effort at all to push in past him.

'I don't do any medical work,' he mumbled, looking at my bandaged arm. 'Not for police stoolies I don't, so get the hell lost.'

'Your conversation is both dull and repetitious,' I told him, because it was. 'I am here to offer you a strictly legitimate business deal with value given for money received. The mere fact that it happens to be illegal should bother neither of us. Least of all you.' I ignored his mumbled protests and looked into the next room. 'According to information of great reliability you live here in unmarried bliss with a girl named Zina. What I have to say is not for her undoubtedly shell-like ears. Where is she?'

'Out!' he shouted. 'And you too, out!' He clutched a tall bottle by the neck and raised it threateningly.

'Would you like that?' I asked and dropped a thick wad of fresh bank notes on the table. 'And that – and that –' I followed with two more bundles. The bottle slipped from his loose fingers and fell to the floor while his eyes bulged out further and further as if they were on pistons. I added a few more bundles to the pile until I had his undivided attention.

It really didn't take much discussion. Once he had assured himself that I really meant to go through with the proposition it was just a matter of settling the details. The money had an instantly sobering effect on him, and though he had a tendency to twitch and vibrate there was nothing wrong with his reasoning powers.

'Just one last problem,' I said as I started to leave. 'What about the worthy Zina – are you going to tell her about this?'

'You crazy?' Vulff asked with undisguised surprise.

'I suppose that means you won't tell her. Since only you and I are going to know about this operation, how are you going to explain your absence or where the money has come from?'

This was even more shocking to him. 'Explain? To *her*? She isn't going to see either me or the money once I leave here. Which will be no more than ten minutes from now.'

'I see,' I said, and I did. I also thought it was rather uncharitable of him since the unlucky Zina had been supporting him by practicing a trade that most women shun. I made a mental note to see what could be done to even the score a little. In the future though. Right now I had to see to the dissolution of James Bolivar diGriz.

Sparing no expense I ordered all the surgical and operating room equipment that Vulff could suggest. Whenever possible I bought robot-controlled devices since he would be working alone. Everything was loaded in a heavy carrier rented for the occasion and we drove out to the house in the country together.

Neither of us would trust the other out of his sight which was of course understandable. Financial payments were the hardest to arrange since the pure-hearted Dr Vulff was sure I would bash in his skull and take back all of my money once the job was finished – never realizing of course that as long as there were banks I would never be broke. The safeguards were finally arranged to his satisfaction and we began our solitary and important business.

The house was lonely and self-contained, perched on the cliff above a far reach of the lake. What fresh food we needed was delivered once a week, along with the mail which consisted of drugs and other medical supplies. The operations began.

Modern surgical techniques being what they are there was of course no pain or shock. I was confined to bed and at times was loaded with so much sedation that days passed in a dreamy fog. Between two periods of radical surgery I took the precaution of seeing that a sleeping pill was included in Vulff's evening drink. This drink was of course non-alcoholic since his traveling this entire course mounted on the water wagon was one of the conditions of our agreement. Whenever he found it difficult I restored his resolution with a little more money. All this continence had his nerves on edge and I thought he would appreciate a good night's sleep. I also wanted to do a little investigating. When I was sure he was deeply under I picked the lock of his door and searched his room.

I suppose the gun was there as a matter of insurance, but you can never tell with these nervous types. My days of being a target were over if I had anything to say about it. The gun was a pocket model of a recoilless .50, neat and deadly. The mechanism worked fine and the cartridges still held all their deadly power, but there would be some difficulty in shooting the thing after I filed off the end of the firing pin.

Finding the camera was no shock since I have very little faith left in the basic wholesomeness of mankind. That I was his benefactor and financer wasn't enough for Vulff. He was lining up some blackmail just in case. There was plenty of exposed film, no doubt filled with studies of my unconcious face Before and After. I put all the film, including the unexposed rolls, under the x-ray machine for a nice long treatment and that settled that.

Vulff did a good job in the times when he wasn't moaning about the absence of spirituous beverages or nubile females. Bending and shortening my femurs altered my height and walk. Hands, face, skull, ears – all of these were changed permanently to build a new individual. Skillful use of the correct hormones caused a change in the pigment cells, darkening the natural color of my skin and hair, even altering the hair pattern itself. The last thing done, when Vulff's skill was at its peak, was a delicate touch on my vocal cords that deepened and roughened my speech.

When it was all finished Slippery Jim diGriz was dead and Hans Schmidt was born. Not a very inspired name I admit, but it was just designed to cover the period before I shed Vulff and began my important enterprise.

'Very good, very good indeed,' I said, looking into the mirror and watching my fingers press a stranger's face.

'God, I could use a drink,' Vulff gasped behind me, sitting on his already-packed bags. He had been hitting the medical alcohol the last few days, until I had spiked it with my favorite regurgitant, and he was nervously anxious to get back to some heavy drinking. 'Give me the balance of the money that's due and let's get out of here!'

'Patience, doctor,' I murmured and slipped him the packet of bills. He broke the bank wrapper and began to count them with quick, caressing touches of his fingers. 'Waste of time doing that,' I told him, but he kept right on. 'I've taken the liberty of writing "STOLEN" on each bill, with ink that will fluoresce when the bank puts it under the ultraviolet.'

This stopped the counting all right, and drained him white at the same instant. I ought to warn him about the old ticker, that's the way he would pop off if he didn't watch out.

'What do you mean, stolen?' he choked after a bit.

'Well they were, you know. All of the money I paid you with was stolen.' His face went even whiter and I was sure he would never reach fifty, not with circulation like that. 'You shouldn't let it worry you. The other stuff was all in old bills. I've passed a lot of it without any trouble.'

'But . . . *why*?' he finally squeezed out.

'Sensible question, doctor. I've sent the same amount – in untampered bills, of course – to your old friend Zina. I felt you owed her that much at least, after all she had done for you. Fair is fair you know.'

He glared at me while I tossed all the machines, surgical supplies and such off the cliff. I was careful not to have my back to him when he was too close; other than this all the precautions had already been taken. When I glanced up by chance and saw that a covert smile had replaced the earlier expression, I knew it was time to reveal the rest of my arrangements.

'An air cab will be here in a few minutes; we'll leave together. I regret to inform you that there won't be enough time after we arrive in Freiburbad for you to seek out Zina and thrash her as planned, and get the money back.' His guilty start proved that he was really an amateur at this sort of thing. I continued, hoping he would be grateful for this complete revelation of how to do things in an efficient criminal manner. 'I've timed everything rather carefully from here on in. Today is a bit unusual in that there are two starships leaving the port within minutes of each other. I've booked a ticket on one for myself – here is your ticket on the other. I've paid in advance for it, though I don't expect you to thank me.' He took the ticket with all the spirited interest of an old maid picking up a dead snake. 'The need for speed – if you will pardon the rhyme – is urgent. A few minutes after your ship leaves an envelope will be delivered to the police describing your part in this operation.'

Dear Doctor Vulff digested all this as we waited for the copter to arrive, and from his sickening expression I saw he could find no flaws in the arrangements. During the entire flight he huddled away from me in his chair and never said a word. Without a bon voyage or even a curse he made for his ship upon our arrival and I watched him board it. I of course merely went in the direction of mine and turned off before entering it. I had as much intention of leaving Freibur as I had of informing the police that an illegal operation had taken place. The last thing I wanted was attention. Both little lies had merely been devices to make sure that the alcoholic doctor went away and stayed away before he began his solitary journey to cirrhosis. There was no reason for me to leave, in fact every reason for me to stay.

Angelina was still on this planet, and I wanted no interference while I tracked her down.

Perhaps it was presumptuous of me to be positive, yet I felt I knew Angelina very well by this time. Our crooked little minds rotated in many of the same cycles of dishonesty. Up to a certain point I felt I could predict her reactions with firm logic. Firstly – she would be very happy about my bloody destruction. She got the same big bang out of corpses that most girls get from new clothes. Thinking me dead would make following her that much easier. I knew she would take normal precautions against the police and other agents of the Corps. But they wouldn't know she was on Freibur – there was nothing to connect my death with her presence. Therefore she didn't have to run again, but could stay on this planet under a new cover and changed personality. That she would want to stay here I had very little doubt. Freibur was a planet that seemed designed for illegal operation. In my years of knocking around the known universe I had never before come up against a piece of fruit so ripe for plucking. A heady mixture of the old and the new. In the old, caste-ridden, feudalistic Freibur a stranger would have been instantly recognized and watched. On the modern League planets computers, mechanization, robots and an ever-vigilant police force left very little room for illegal operations. It was only when these two different cultures are mixed and merged that imaginative operations became really possible.

This planet was peaceful enough; you had to give the League societies experts credit for that much. Before they brought in the first antibiotic pill or punch-card computer, they saw to it that law and order were firmly instituted. Nevertheless the opportunities were still there if you knew where to look. Angelina knew where to look and so did I.

Except – after weeks of futile investigation – I finally faced the brutal fact that we were both looking for different things. I can't deny the time was spent pleasantly since I uncovered countless opportunities for fine jobs and lucrative capers. If it hadn't been for the pressure of finding Angelina I do believe I could have had the time of my life in this crook's paradise. This pleasure was denied me because the pressure to catch up with Angelina nagged at me constantly like an aching tooth.

Finding intuition wanting I tried mechanical means. Hiring the best computer available, I fed entire libraries into its memory circuits and set it countless problems. In the course of this kilowatt-consuming business I became an expert on the economy of Freibur, but in the end was no closer to finding Angelina than I had been when I started. She had a driving urge for power and control, but I had no idea in what way it would find its outlet. There were many economic solutions I turned up for grabbing the reins of Freibur society, but investigation showed that she was involved in none of these. The King – Villelm IX – seemed the obvious pressure point for actual physical control of the planet. A complete investigation of Vill, his family and close royal relatives, turned up some juicy scandal but no Angelina. I was stopped dead.

While drowning my sorrows in a bottle of distilled spirits the solution to this dilemma finally struck me. Admittedly I was sodden with drink at the time, yet the paralysis of my neural axons was undoubtedly the source of the idea. Any man that says he thinks better drunk than sober is a fool. But this was a different case altogether. I was feeling, not thinking, and my anger at her escape cracked the lid off my more civilized impulses. I choked a pillow to death imagining it was her neck and finally shouted, 'Crazy, crazy, that's her trouble, all the way around the bend and dotty as polka-dots!' When I fell onto the bed everything swooped around and around in sickening circles and I mumbled, 'Just plain crazy. I would have to be crazy myself to figure out which way she will jump next.' With this my eyes closed and I fell asleep. While the words swam down through the alcohol-saturated layers until they reached a deeper level where a spark of rationality still dwelled.

When they hit bottom I was wide awake and sitting up in bed, struck dumb by the ghastly truth. It would require all the conviction I had – and a little more – to do it.

I would have to follow her down the path of insanity if I wanted to find her.

CHAPTER
-13-

In the cold light of morning the idea didn't look any more attractive – or any less true. I could do it, or not do it, as I chose. There could be no doubting the wild tinge of insanity that colored Angelina's life. Every one of our contacts had been marked by a ruthless indifference to human life. She killed with coldness or with pleasure – as when she had shot me – but always with total disregard for people. I doubt if even she had any idea of how many murders she had committed in her lifetime. By her standards I was a rank amateur. I hadn't killed more than – that kind of violence was rarely necessary in my type of operation – surely no more than . . . none?

Well, well – old chicken-hearted revealed at last. Rough and tough diGriz the killer who never killed! It was nothing to be ashamed of, quite the opposite in fact. I placed a value on human life, the one unchanging value in existence. Angelina valued herself and her desires, and nothing else. To follow her down the twisted path of her own making I would have to place myself in the same mental state that she lived in.

This is not as difficult as it sounds – at least in

theory. I have had some experience with the psychoto-mimetic drugs and was well aware of their potency. Centuries of research have produced drugs that can simulate any mental condition in the user. Like to be paranoid for a day? Take a pill. You can go around the bend, friend. It is a matter of record that people have actually tried these concoctions for kicks, but *that* bored with life I don't want to be. There would have to be a lot stronger reason before I would subject my delicate gray cells to this kind of jarring around. Like finding Angelina, for instance.

About the only good thing about these pixilation producers is the accepted fact that the effects are only temporary. When the drug wears off so do the hallucinations. I hoped. Nowhere in the texts I studied did they mention a devil's brew such as the one I was concocting. It was a laborious task hunting down all of Angelina's fascinating symptoms in the textbooks and trying to fit them to an inclusive psychotic pattern. I even called in some professional help to aid analyzing her case, not mentioning, of course, to what use I intended to put the information. In the end I had a bottle of slightly smoky liquid and a taped recording of autohypnotic suggestions to play into my ears while the shot was taking effect. All that remained was screwing my courage to the sticking-place as they say in the classics. Not really all that remained – I wanted to take some precautions first. I rented a room in a cheap hotel and left orders not to be disturbed at any time. This was the first time I had ever tried this particular type of nonsense and since I had no idea of how foggy my memory would be I left a few notes around to remind me of the job. After a half day of this kind of preparation I realized I was making excuses.

'Well it's not easy to deliberately go insane,' I told my rather pale reflection in the mirror. The reflection agreed but that didn't stop either of us from rolling up our sleeves and filling large hypodermic needles with murky madness.

'Here's looking at you,' I said, and slipped the needle gently in the vein and slowly pushed the plunger home.

The results were anticlimactic to say the least. Outside of a ringing in my ears and a twinge of headache that quickly passed I felt nothing. I knew better than to go out though, so I read the newspaper for a while, until I felt tired. The whole thing seemed a little foolish and pretty much of a letdown. I went to sleep with the tape player whispering softly in my ears much ego-building epigrams as, 'You are better than everyone else and you know it, and people who don't know it had better watch out,' and 'They are all fools and if you were in charge things would be different, and why *aren't* you in charge, it's easy enough.'

Waking up was uncomfortable because of the pain in my ears where the earphones were still plugged in, my own stupid voice droning away at me. Nothing had changed and the whole futile experiment was a waste and waste makes me angry. The earphones broke in my hands and I felt better, felt much better still when I had stamped the tape player into a tangle of rubble.

My face rasped when I ran my hand over it; I had been days without a shave. Rubbing in the dip cream I looked into the mirror over the sink and an odd fact struck me for the first time. This new face fitted me a lot better than the old one. A fault of birth or the ugliness of my parents – whom I hated deeply, the only right thing they ever did was to produce me – had given me a face that didn't fit my personality. The new one was better, handsomer for one thing and a lot stronger. I should have thanked that fumble-finger quack Vulff for producing a masterpiece. I should have thanked him with a bullet. That would guarantee that no one would ever be able to trace me through him. It must have been a warm day and I was suffering a fever when I let him get safely away like that.

On the table was a piece of paper with a single word written on it, my own handwriting though I can't imagine why the hell I left it there. *Angelina* it said. Angelina, how I would love to get that tender white throat between my hands and squeeze until your eyeballs popped. Hah! I had to laugh at the thought, made a funny picture indeed. Yet I shouldn't be so flippant about it. Angelina was important. I was going to find her and nothing was going to stop me. She had made a fool of me and had tried to kill me. If anyone deserved to die it was her. It was an awful waste in some ways yet it had to be done. I shredded the note into fine pieces.

All at once the room was very oppressing and I wanted out. What made me doubly angry was the fact the key was missing. I remember taking it out, but had no idea where I had put it. The slob at the desk was slow at answering and I was tempted to tell him just what I thought of the service, but I refrained. There is only one permanent cure for these types. A spare key rattled into the basket of the pneumo and I let myself out. I needed some food and I needed some drink and most of all I needed a quiet place for some thought.

A nearby spot provided all three – after I had chased the hookers away. They were all dogs, and Angelina just playing a role had been better than this entire crowd lumped together. Angelina. She was on my mind tonight with a vengeance. The drinks warmed my gut and Angelina warmed my memory. To think that I had actually once considered turning her in or possibly killing her. What a waste! The only intelligent woman I had ever run across. And all woman – I'll never forget the way she walked in that dress. Once she had been tamed a bit – what a team we could make! This thought was so mentally aphrodisiac that my skin burned and I drained my glass at a single swallow.

Something had to be done; I had to find her. She would never have left a ripe plum of a planet like this one. A girl with her ambition could go right to the top here, nothing could stop her. And that's of course where she would be – eventually if not now. She must spend her life feeling damned because she was a woman, knowing she was better than the rest of the cruds around, then proving it to herself and them over and over again. My arrival would be the biggest favor Angelina could have. I didn't have to prove myself better than the hicks on this rubiefied planet – just one look did that. When Angelina hooked up with me she could stop fighting, relax and take orders. The contest would be over for all time.

While I sat there something was nagging at me, some vital fact I had to remember – yet couldn't. For a second I fumbled with the memory before I realized what it was. The injection would be wearing off soon! I had to get back to the room, quickly. There had been some fear about the danger of this business, but I realized now that was just my earlier cowardice. This stuff was no more dangerous than aspirin. And at the same time it was the galaxy's greatest pick-up. New worlds of possibilities were opening up to me, my mind was clearer and my thoughts more logical. I wasn't going back to the old muddled-head stuff. At the bar I paid the bartender, my fingers tapping impatiently while he slothfully made change for me.

'A wiseguy?' I asked, loud enough for everyone in the joint to hear. 'A customer is in a hurry so that's your chance to shortchange him. This is two gilden short.' I held the money out in my palm and when he bent to count it I came up quick with the hand and let him have the whole thing right in the face, bills, coins, thumb and fingers. At the same time I told him – in a low voice so no one else could hear – just what I thought of him. Freibur slang is rich in insult and I used the best on him. I could have done more but I was in a hurry to get back to the hotel room, and teaching him a lesson would take time. When I turned to go I kept an eye behind me in a mirror across the room and it's a good thing I did. He pulled a length of pipe out from under the bar and raised it over my head. Of course I stood still to give him a nice target and not throw off his aim – only stepping aside as the arm came down, just moving enough to let the pipe skin by me.

It was no trick at all to grab the arm, keep it going down, and break the bone across the edge of the bar. The screams were heart-warming to say the least, and I only wish I had the time to stay and really give him something to scream about. There was just no time left.

'You saw him viciously attack me,' I told the stunned customers as I headed for the door. Rough-and-tough had slumped down and was moaning out of sight somewhere behind the bar. 'I'm going to call the police now – see that he doesn't leave.' Of course he had as much intention of leaving as I had of calling the law. I was out the door long before any of them had made their minds up as to just what was going on.

Of course I couldn't run and draw any attention to myself. Getting back to the hotel at a fast walk was the best I could do, but I was sweating all over from the tension. Inside the room the first thing I saw was the container on the table, with the needle wrapped in cloth beside it. My hands didn't shake, but they would have if I had let them. This was a very close thing.

Collapsed in a chair afterwards I held up the jar and saw that there was less than a milliliter of juice left. The very next thing on the agenda was the necessity of laying in a supply of the stuff. I could remember the formula clearly and would have no trouble rebuilding it. Of course there would be no drug suppliers open at this time of night, but that made things a lot easier. There is a law of history that says weapons were invented before money. In my suitcase was a recoilless .75 that could get me more of the galaxy's goods than all of the money in existence.

That was my mistake. Some nagging worry gnawed me then but I ignored it. The tension and then the relief after getting the shot had me all loosened up. On top of that was the need to hurry, the limited time I had to find what I needed and get it back to the hotel room. My thoughts were on the job and how best to do it as I unlocked the suitcase and reached for my gun lying right there on top of the clothes. At this point the thin voice in my memory was screaming inaudibly to me, but this only made me reach faster for the gun. Something was badly wrong and this was the thing that would fix it. As I grabbed the butt the memory broke through ... just a little bit too slow.

Dropping the gun I dived for the door, too late by far. Behind me I heard a pop as the sleep-gas grenade I had put under the gun let go. Even as I fell forward into darkness I wondered how I could ever have possibly done such a stupid thing as that ...

CHAPTER
−14−

Coming out of the gas, my first feeling was one of regret. It is a truism that the workings of the mind are a source of constant astonishment. The effects of my devil's brew had worn off. There was nothing wrong with my memory, now that the posthypnotic blocks I had put on it had been removed. All too vividly I could recall the details of my interlude of madness. Though I sickened at the things I had thought and done, I simultaneously felt a twinge of regret that could not be abolished. There had been terrible freedom in standing so alone that even the lives of other men meant less than nothing. Undoubtedly a warped sensation, but still a tremendously attractive one. Like taking drugs. Even while detesting the thought I felt the desire for more of the same.

In spite of my twelve hours of forced sleep I was exhausted. It took all of my energy to drag over to the bed and collapse on it. Foresight had provided a bottle of stimulating spirits and I poured a glassful. Sipping at this I tried to put my mental house in order, not a very easy task. I have read many times about the cesspool of dark desires that lies in our subconscious minds, but this was the first time I had ever had mine stirred up. It was quite revealing to examine some of the things that had floated to the surface.

My attitude towards Angelina needed a good looking at. The most important fact I had to face was the strong attraction I felt for her. Love? Put any name to it you want – I suppose love will do as well as any, though this was no throbbing adolescent passion. I wasn't blind to her faults, in fact I rather detested them now that I knew her murderously amoral existence had an echo in my own mind. But logic and convictions have very little to do with emotions. Hating this side of her didn't remove the attraction of a personality so similar to my own. I echoed my psychotic self's attitude – what a team we might have made! This was of course impossible, but that didn't stop me from wanting it. Love and hate are reputed to be very close and in my case they were certainly rubbing shoulders. And the whole confused business wasn't helped in the slightest by the fact that Angelina was so damnably attractive. I took a long drag at my drink.

Finding her should be easy now. The carelessness with which I took this for granted was a little shocking. I had gained no new information while mentally aberrant. Just a great chunk of insight the tortured grooves that my Angelina's mind trundled along. There could be no doubt that raw power was what she desired. This couldn't be obtained through influencing the king, I saw this now. Violence was the way, a power putsch, perhaps assassination, certainly revolution and turmoil of some kind. This had been the pattern in the bad old days on Freibur when sovereignty had been the prize of battle. Any of the nobility could be crowned, and whenever the old king's grip weakened it was a cue for a power struggle that would produce the new monarch. Of course that sort of thing had stopped as soon as the societics specialists from the League worked their little tricks.

The old days were on the way back – that was clear. Angelina was going to see this world bathed in blood and death to satisfy her own ambition. She was out there now – somewhere – grooming the man for the job. One of the counts, still very important in the semi-feudal economy, was having his ego inflated and guided by a new power behind the throne. This is the pattern Angelina had used before, and would be sure to use again. There could be no doubt.

Only one small factor was missing. Who was the man?

My dive into the depths of self-analysis had left a definitely unwholesome taste in my mouth that no amount of liquor could wash away. What I needed was a little touch of action to tone up my drooping nerve ends and accelerate my sluggish blood. Tracking down Angelina's front man would be just the charge my battery needed. Merely thinking about it helped, and it was with eagerness that I searched the newspaper for the Court News column. There was a Grand Ball just two days distant, the perfect cover for this operation.

For these two days I was kept busy on the many small tasks that put the polish of perfection on a job like this. Any boob can crash a party, in fact usually does, since that is all one seems to meet at this kind of affair. It takes a unique talent like mine to construct a cover personality that is unshakeable. Research supplied me with a homeland, a distant province poor in everything except a thick dialect that provided the base for most Freibur jokes. Because of these inherent handicaps the populace of Misteldross was noted for its pugnacity and general bullheadedness. There were minor nobility there who no one took much notice of, or kept any records about, enabling me to adopt the cover of Grav Bent Diebstall. The family name meant either bandit or tax-gatherer in the local dialect, which gives you an idea of the kind of economy they had had, as well as the source of the family title. A military tailor cut me a dress uniform and while I was being fitted I memorized great chunks of the family history to bore people with. I saw where I could be the life of any party.

Another thing I did was to send off a thick wad of money to the maimed bartender, who was now working with the handicap of having his arm in a cast. He really had short-changed me, but his suffering was entirely out of proportion to this minor crime. My anonymous gift was strictly conscience money and I felt much better after having done it.

A moonlight visit to the royal printers supplied an invitation to the party. My uniform fitted like a sausage skin, my boots gleamed enthusiastically and I was one of the first guests to arrive since the royal table had a tremendous reputation and work had increased my appetite. I crashed and clattered wonderfully when I bowed to the King – spurs and sword, they go all the way with the archaic nonsense on Freibur – and looked at him closely while he mumbled something inaudible. His eyes were glassy and unfocused and I realized there was some truth in the rumor that he always got stoned on his private bottle before coming to one of these affairs. Apparently he hated crowds and parties and much preferred to putter with his bugs – he was an amateur entomologist of no small talents. I passed on to the queen who was much more receptive. She was twenty years his junior and attractive in a handsomely inflated, bovine way. Rumor also had it that she was bored by his beetles and much preferred homo sapiens to lepidoptera. I tested this calumny by giving her hand an extra little squeeze when I held it and queeny squeezed back with an expression of great interest. I moved on to the buffet.

While I ate, the guests continued to arrive. Watching them as they entered didn't interfere with my demolishing the food or sampling all of the wines. I had finished stoking up by the time the rest were just starting, so I could circulate among them. All of the women were subjected to my very close scrutiny, and most of them enjoyed it because, if I say so myself, with my new face and the fit of the uniform I cut a mean swath through the local types. I really wasn't expecting to run across Angelina's trail this easily, but there was always the chance. Only a few of the women even remotely resembled her, but it took only a few words each time to settle the fact that they were true-blue blue-blood and not my little interstellar killer. This task was made simpler by the fact that the Freibur beauties ran heavily towards the flesh, and Angelina was a neat and petite package. I went back to the bar.

'You have been given a Royal Command,' an adenoidal voice said in my ear while fingers plucked at my sleeve. I turned and gave my best scowl to the character who still clutched the fabric.

'Let go the suit or I push your buck-toothed face the punch bowl in,' I growled in my thickest Misteldrossian accent. He let go as if he had grabbed something hot and got all red and excited-looking. 'That's better,'

I added, cutting off his next words. 'Now – who wants to see me – the King?'

'Her majesty, the Queen,' he managed to squeeze out between thin lips.

'That's good. I want to see her too. Show the way.' I forged a way through the crowd while my new friend clattered behind, trying to pass me. I stopped before I reached the group around Queen Helda and let him get ahead all out of breath and sweating.

'Your majesty, this is the Baron—'

'Grav not Baron,' I cut in with my hideously rich accent. 'Grav Bent Diebstall from a poor provincial family, cheated centuries ago of our rightful title by thieving and jealous counts.' I scowled straight at my guide as if he had been in the plot and he turned the flush on again.

'I don't recognize all of your honors, Grav Bent,' the Queen said in her low voice that reminded me of pastures on a misty morn. She pointed to my manly chest, to the row of decorations I had purchased from a curio dealer just that morning.

'Galactic medals, your majesty. A younger son of the provincial nobility, his family impoverished by the greedy and corrupt, can find little opportunity to advance himself here on Freibur. That is way I took service offplanet and served for the best years of my youth in the Stellar Guard. These are for commonplace happenings such as battles, invasions and space boardings. But *this* is the one I can really take pride in—' I fingered through the jingling hardware until I came to an unsightly thing, all comets, novas and sparkling lights. 'This is the Stellar Star, the most prized award in the Guards.' I took it in my hand and gave it a long look. In fact I think it *was* a Guard decoration, given out for reenlisting or five years of K. P. or some such.

'It's beautiful,' the Queen said. Her taste in medals was no better than her taste in clothes, but what can you expect on these backward planets.

'It is that,' I agreed. 'I don't enjoy describing the medal's history, but if it is a royal command . . . ?' It was, and given very coyly indeed. I lied about my exploits for awhile and kept them all interested. There would be plenty of talk about me in the morning and I hoped some of it would trickle down to Angelina's ears, wherever she was hiding. Thinking of her took the edge off my fun, and I managed to excuse myself and go back to the bar.

I spent the rest of the evening talking up the wonders of my imaginary history to everyone I could nail. Most of them seemed to enjoy it, since the court was normally short on laughs. The only one who didn't seem to be getting a charge out of it was myself. Though the plan had seemed good at first, the more I became involved with it the slower it appeared. I might flutter around the fringe of these fantastically dull court circles for months without finding a lead to Angelina. The process had to be accelerated. There was one idea drifting in and out of my head, but it bordered on madness. If it misfired I would be either dead or barred from these noble circles forever. This last was a fate I could easily stand – but it wouldn't help me find my lovely quarry. However – if the plan did work it would shortcut all the other nonsense. I flipped a coin to decide, and of course won since I had palmed the coin before the toss. It was going to be action.

Before coming I had pocketed a few items that might

come in handy during the course of the evening. One of them was a sure-fire introduction to the King in case I felt that getting nearer to him might be of some importance. I slipped this into an outer pocket, filled the largest glass I could find with sweet wine, and trundled through the cavernous rooms in search of my prey.

If King Villelm had been crocked when he arrived, he was now almost paralyzed. He must have had a steel bar sewn into the back of his white uniform jacket because I swear his own spine shouldn't have held him up. But he was still drinking and swaying back and forth, his head bobbing as though it were loosely attached. He had a crowd of old boys around him and they must have been swapping off-color stories because they gave me varying degrees of get-lost looks when I trundled up and snapped to attention. I was bigger than most of them and must have made a nice blob of color because I caught Villy's eye and the head slowly slewed around in my direction. One of his octogenarian cronies had met me earlier in the evening and was forced to make the introduction.

'A very great pleasure to meet your majesty,' I droned with a bit of a drunken blur to my voice. Not that the King noticed, but some of the others did and scowled. 'I am by way of being a bit of an entomologist myself, if you will pardon the expression, hoping to follow in your royal footsteps. I am keen on this and feel that greater attention should be paid on Freibur, more respect given I should say, and more opporunity taken to utilize the advantageous aspects of the forminifera, lepidoptera and all the others. Heraldry, for instance, the flags might utilize the more visual aspects of insects ...'

I babbled on like this for a while, the crowd getting impatient with the unwanted interruption. The King – who wasn't getting in more than one word in ten – got tired of nodding after a while and his attention began to wander. My voice thickened and blurred and I could see them wondering how to get rid of the drunk. When the first tentative hand reached out for my elbow I played my trump card.

'Because of your majesty's interest,' I said, fumbling in my pocket, 'I carefully kept this specimen, carrying it across countless light years to reach its logical resting place, your highness's collection.' Pulling out the flat plastic case, I held it under his nose. With an effort he blinked his watery eyes back into focus and let out a little gasp. The others crowded around and I gave them a few seconds to enjoy the thing.

Well it was a beautiful bug, I can't deny that. However it had not traveled across countless light years because I had just made it myself that morning. Most of the parts were assembled from other insects, with a few pieces of plastic thrown in where nature had let me down. Its body was as long as my hand, and it had three sets of wings, each set in a different color. There were a lot of legs underneath, pretty mismatched I'm afraid since they came from a dozen other insects and a lot of them got mashed or misplaced during construction. Some other nice touches like a massive stinger, three eyes, a corkscrew tail and such-like were not lost on my rapt audience. I had had the foresight to make the case of tinted plastic which blurred the contents nicely and hinted at rather than revealed them.

'But you must see it more closely, your highness,' I said, snapping open the case while both of us swayed back and forth. This was a difficult juggling act as I had to hold the case in the same hand as my wine glass, leaving my other hand free to grasp the monstrosity. I plucked it out between thumb and forefinger and the king leaned close, the drink in his own glass slopping back and forth in his eagerness. I squeezed just a bit with my thumb and the bug popped forward in lively fashion and dived into the King's glass.

'Save it! Save it!' I cried. 'A valuable specimen!' I plunged my fingers in after it and chased it around and around. Some of the drink slopped out staining Villelm's gilt-edged cuff. A gasp went up and angry voices sounded. Someone pulled hard at my shoulder.

'Leave off you title-stealing clots!' I shouted, and pulled away roughly from the grasp. The drowned insect flew out of my fingers and landed on the King's chest, from where it fell slowly to the floor, shedding wings, legs and other parts on the way. I must have used a very inferior glue. When I leaped to grab the dropping corpse the forgotten drink in my other hand splashed red and sticky onto the King's jacket. A howl of anger went up from the crowd.

I'll say this much for the King, he took it well. Stood there swaying like a tree in the storm, but offering no protest outside of mumbling, 'I say … I say …' a few times. Not even when I rubbed the wine in with my handkerchief, treading on his toes by accident as the crowd behind pushed too close. One of them pulled hard at my arm, then let go when I shrugged. My arm struck against Villelm IX's noble chest and his royal upper plate popped out on the floor to add to the fun.

Fun it was too, once the old boys got cleared away. The younger nobility leaped to their majesty's defense and I showed them a thing or two about mix-it-up fighting that I had learned on a number of planets. They made up in energy what they lacked in technique and we had a really good go-around. Women screamed, strong men cursed and the King was half carried out of the fracas. After that things got dirty and I did too. I couldn't blame them, but that didn't stop me from giving just as good as I received.

My last memory is of a number of them holding me while another one hit me. I got him in the face with the shoe on my free leg, but they grabbed that too and his replacement turned off all the lights.

CHAPTER
–15–

Uncivilized as my behaviour had been, the jailers persisted in treating me in a most civilized fashion. I grumbled about this and made their job as hard as possible. I hadn't voluntarily entered prison in order to win a popularity contest. Pulling all those gags on the poor old King had been a risk. *Lèse-majesté* is the sort of crime that is usually punishable by death. Happily the civilizing influences of the League had penetrated darkest Freibur, and the locals now fell over backwards to show me how law-abiding they were. I would have none of it. When they brought me a meal I ate it, then destroyed the dishes to show my contempt for this unlawful detention.

This was the bait. The bruises I had suffered would be a small enough price to pay if my attempt at publicity paid off in the right quarters. Without a doubt I was being discussed. A figure of shame, a traitor to my class. A violent man in a peaceful world, and a pugnacious, combative uncompromising one at that. In short I was all the things a good Freiburian detested, and the sort of a man Angelina should have a great deal of interest in.

In spite of its recent bloody past, Freibur was

woefully short of roughneck manpower. Not at the very lowest levels of course; the portside drinkeries were stuffed with musclebound apes with pinhead brains. Angelina would be able to recruit all of those she needed. But strongarm squads alone wouldn't win her a victory. She needed allies and aid from the nobility, and from what I had seen this sort of talent was greatly lacking. In my indirect manner I had displayed all the traits she would be interested in, doing it in such a way that she wouldn't know the show had been arranged only for her. The trap was open, all she had to do was step into it.

Metal boomed as the turnkey rapped on the door. 'You have visitors, Grav Diebstall,' he said, opening the inner grill.

'Tell them to go to hell!' I shouted. 'There's no one on this poxy planet I want to see.'

Paying no attention to my request, he bowed in the governor of the prison and a pair of ancient types wearing black clothes and severe looks. I did the best I could do ignore them. They waited grimly until the guard had gone, then the skinniest opened a folder he was carrying and slowly drew out a sheet of paper with his fingertips.

'I will not sign a suicide note so you can butcher me in my sleep,' I snarled at him. This rattled him a bit, but he tried to ignore it.

'That is an unfair suggestion,' he intoned solemnly. 'I am the Royal Attorney and would never condone such an action.' All three of them nodded together as though they were pulled by one string, and the effect was so compulsive that I almost nodded myself.

'I will not commit suicide voluntarily,' I said harshly

to break the spell of agreement. 'That is the last word that will be said on the subject.'

The Royal Attorney had been around the courts long enough not to be thrown off his mark by this kind of obliquity. He coughed, rattled the paper, and got back to basics.

'There are a number of crimes you could be charged with young man,' he droned, with an intensely gloomy expression draped on his face. I yawned, unimpressed. 'I hope this will not have to be done,' he went on, 'since it would only cause harm to all concerned. The King himself does not wish to see this happen, and in fact has pressed upon me his earnest desire to have this affair ended quietly now. His desire for peace has prevailed upon us all, and I am here now to put his wish into action. If you will sign this apology, you will be placed aboard a starship leaving tonight. The matter will be ended.'

'Trying to get rid of me to cover up your drunken brawls at the palace, hey?' I sneered. The Attorney's face purpled but he controlled his temper with a magnificent effort. If they threw me off the planet now everything was wasted.

'You are being insulting, sir!' he snorted. 'You are not without blame in this matter, remember. I heartily recommended that you accept the King's leniency in this tragic affair and sign the apology.' He handed the paper to me and I tore it to pieces.

'Apologize? Never!' I shouted at them. 'I was merely defending my honor against your drunken louts and larcenous nobility, all descended from thieves who stole the titles rightly belonging to my family!'

They left then, and the prison governor was the only one young and sturdy enough for me to help on the way with the toe of my shoe in the appropriate spot. Everything was as it should be. The door clanged shut behind them – on a rebellious, cantankerous, belligerent son of the Freibur soil. I had arranged things perfectly to bring me to the attention of Angelina. But unless she became interested in me soon I stood a good chance of spending the rest of my days behind these grim walls.

Waiting has always been bad for my nerves. I am a thinker during moments of peace, but a man of action most of the time. It is one thing to prepare a plan and leap boldy into it. It is another thing altogether to sit around a grubby prison cell wondering if the plan has worked or if there is a weak link in the chain of logic.

Should I crack out of this pokey? That shouldn't be hard to do, but it had better be saved for a last resort. Once out I would have to stay undercover and there would be no chance of her contacting me. That was why I was gnawing my way through all my fingernails. The next move was up to Angelina; all I could do was wait. I only hoped that she would gather the right conclusions from all the violent evidence I had supplied.

After a week I was stir-crazy. The Royal Attorney never came back and there was no talk of a trial or sentencing. I had presented them with an annoying problem, and they must have been scratching their heads feebly over it and hoping I would go away. I almost did. Getting out of this backwoods jail would have been simplicity itself. But I was waiting for a message from my deadly love. I toyed with the possibilities of the things she might do. Perhaps arrange pressure through the court to have me freed? Or smuggle in a file and a note to see if I could break out on my own? This second possibility appealed to me most and I shredded my bread every time it arrived to see if anything had been baked into it. There was nothing.

On the eighth day Angelina made her play, in the most forthright manner of her own. It was night, but something unaccustomed woke me up. Listening produced no answers, so I slipped over to the barred opening in the door and saw a most attractive sight at the end of the hall. The night guard was sprawled on the floor and a burly masked figure dressed completely in black stood over him with a cosh in one meaty hand. Another stranger, dressed like the first, came up and they dragged the guard further along the hall towards me. One of them rummaged in his waist wallet and produced a scrap of red cloth that he put between the guard's limp fingers. Then they turned towards my cell and I moved back out of sight, climbing noiselessly into bed.

A key grated in the lock and the lights came on. I sat up blinking, giving a fine imitation of a man waking up.

'Who's there? What do you want?' I asked.

'Up quickly, and get dressed, Diebstall. You're getting out of here.' This was the first thug I had seen, the blackjack still hanging from his hand. I sagged my jaw a bit, then leaped out of bed with my back to the wall.

'Assassins!' I hissed. 'So that's vile King Villy's bright idea, is it? Going to put a rope around my neck and swear I hung myself? Well come on – but don't think it will be easy!'

'Don't be an idiot!' the man whispered. 'And shut the big mouth. We're here to get you out. We're friends.' Two more men, dressed the same way, pushed in behind him, and I had a glimpse of a fourth one in the hall.

'Friends!' I shouted. 'Murderers is more like it! You'll pay dearly for this crime.'

The fourth man, still in the hall, whispered something and they charged me. I wanted a better glimpse of the boss. He was a small man – if he *was* a man. His clothes were loose and bulky, and there was a stocking mask over his entire head. Angelina would be just about that tall. But before I could get a better look the thugs were on me. I kicked one in the stomach and ducked away. This was fighting barroom style and they had all the advantages. Without shoes or a weapon I didn't stand a chance, and they weren't afraid to use their coshes. I tried hard not to smile with victory as they worked me over.

Only reluctantly did I allow myself to be dragged to the place where I wanted to go.

CHAPTER

-16-

Because the pounding on the head had only made me groggy, one of them broke a sleep capsule under my nose and that was that for a while. So of course I had no idea of how far we had traveled or where on Freibur I was. They must have given me the antidote because the next thing I saw was a scrawny type with a hypodermic injector in his hand. He was peeling back my eyelid to look and I slapped his hand away.

'Going to torture me before you kill me, swine!' I said, remembering the role I had to play.

'Don't worry about that,' a deep voice said behind me, 'you are among friends. People who can understand your irritation with the present régime.'

This voice wasn't much like Angelina's. Neither was the burly, sour-faced owner. The medic slid out and left us alone, and I wondered if the plan had slipped up somewhere. Iron-jaw with the beady eyes had a familiar look – I recognized him as one of the Freiburian nobility. I had memorized the lot and looking at his ugly face I dredged up a mnemonic. A midget painted bright red.

'Rdenrundt – The Count of Rdenrundt,' I said, trying to remember what else I had read about him. 'I might believe you were telling me the truth if you weren't his Highness's first cousin. I find it hard to consider that you would steal a man from the royal jail for your own purposes ...'

'It's not important what you believe,' he snapped angrily. He had a short fuse and it took him a moment to get his temper back under control. 'Villelm may be my cousin – that doesn't mean I think he is the perfect ruler for our planet. You talked a lot about your claims to higher rank and the fact that you had been cheated. Did you mean that? Or are you just another parlor windbag? Think well before your answer – you may be committing yourself. There may be other people who feel as you do, that there is change in the wind.'

Impulsive, enthusiastic, that was me. Loyal friend and deadly enemy and just solid guts when it came to a fight. Jumping forward I grabbed his hand and pumped it.

'If you are telling me the truth, then you have a man at your side who will go the whole course. If you are lying to me and this is some trick of the King's – well then, Count, be ready to fight!'

'No need to fight,' he said, extracting his hand with some difficulty from my clutch. 'Not between us at least. We have a difficult course ahead of us, and we must learn to rely upon each other.' He cracked his knuckles and looked glumly out of the window. 'I sincerely hope that I will be able to rely on you. Freibur is a far different world from the one our ancestors ruled. The League has sapped the fight from our people. There are none I can really rely on.'

'There's nothing wrong with the bunch who took

me out of my cell. They seemed to do the job well enough.'

'Muscle!' he spat, and pressed a button on the arm of his chair. 'Thugs with heads of solid stone. I can hire all of those I need. What I need are men who can lead – help me to lead Freibur into its rightful future.'

I didn't mention the man who led the muscle the previous night, the one who had stayed in the corridor. If Rdenrundt wasn't going to talk about Angelina I certainly couldn't bring up the topic. Since he wanted brain not brawn, I decided to give him a little.

'Did you dream up the torn piece of uniform left in the guards hand in the prison? That was a good touch.'

His eyes narrowed a bit when he turned to look at me. 'You're quite observant, Bent,' he said.

'A matter of training,' I told him, trying to be both unassuming and positive at the same time. 'There was this piece of red cloth with a button in the guard's hand, like something he had grabbed in a struggle. Yet all of the men I saw were dressed only in black. Perhaps a bit of misdirection. . . .'

'With each passing moment I'm getting happier that you have joined me,' he said, and showed me all of his ragged teeth in an expression he must have thought was a grin. 'The Old Duke's men wear red livery, as you undoubtedly know ...'

'And the Old Duke is the strongest supporter of Villelm IX,' I finished for him. 'It wouldn't hurt in the slightest if he had a falling out with the King.'

'Not the slightest,' Rdenrundt echoed, and showed me all of his teeth again. I was beginning to dislike him intensely. If this was the front man Angelina had picked for her operation, then he was undoubtedly the best one for the job on the planet. But he was such a puffed-up crumb, with barely enough imagination to appreciate the ideas Angelina was feeding him. Yet I imagine he had the money and the title – and the ambition – which combination she had to have. Once more I wondered where she was.

Something came in through the door and I recoiled, thinking the war was on. It was only a robot, but it made such a hideous amount of hissing and clanking that I wondered what was wrong with it. The Count ordered the ghastly thing to wheel over the bar, as it turned away I saw what could only have been a *chimney* projecting behind one shoulder. There was the distinct odor of coal smoke in the air.

'Does that robot burn *coal*—?' I gurgled.

'It does,' the Count said, pouring us out a pair of drinks. 'It is a perfect example of what is wrong with the Freiburian economy under the gracious rule of Villelm the Incompetent. You don't see any robots like this in the capital!'

'I should hope not,' I gasped, staring bug-eyed at the trickle of steam escaping from the thing, and the stains of rust and coal dust on its plates. 'Of course I've been away a long time . . . things change . . .'

'They don't change fast enough! And don't act galactic-wise with me, Diebstall. I've been to Misteldross and seen how the rubes live. You have no robots at all – much less a contraption like this.' He kicked at the thing in sullen anger and it staggered back a bit, valves clicking open as steam pumped into the leg pistons to straighten it up. 'Two hundred years come next Grundlovsday we will have been in the League, milked dry and pacified by them – and for what? To provide luxuries for the King in Freiburbad. While out here we get a miserable consignment of a few robot brains and some control circuitry. We have to build the rest of the inefficient monsters ourselves. And out in the real sticks where you come from they think robot is a misspelling of a boat that goes with oars!'

He drained his glass and I made no attempt to explain to him the economics of galactic commerce, planetary prestige, or the multifold levels of intercommunication. This lost planet had been cut off from the mainstream of galactic culture for maybe a thousand years, until contact had been reestablished after the Breakdown. They were being eased back into the culture gradually, without any violent repercussions that might upset the process. Sure, a billion robots could be dumped here tomorrow. What good would that do the economy? It was certainly much better to bring in the control units and let the locals build the things for themselves. If they didn't like the final product they could improve the design instead of complaining.

The Count of course didn't see it this way. Angelina had done a nice job of playing upon his prejudices and desires. He was still glaring at the robot when he leaned forward and suddenly tapped a dial on the thing's side.

'Look at that!' he shouted. 'Down to eighty pounds pressure! Next thing you know the thing will be falling on its face and burning the place down. Stoke, you idiot – *stoke*!!'

A couple of relays closed inside the contraption and the robot clanked and put the tray of glasses down. I took a very long drag on my drink and enjoyed the scene. Trundling over to the fireplace – at a slower pace now I'll admit – it opened a door in its stomach and flame belched out. Using the coal scoop in the pail it shoveled in a good portion of anthracite and banged the firedoor shut again. Rich black smoke boiled from its chimney. At least it was housebroken and didn't shake out its grate here.

'Outside, dammit, outside!' the Count shouted, coughing at the same time. The smoke was a little thick. I poured another drink and decided right then that I was going to like Rdenrundt.

I would have liked it a lot better if I could have found Angelina. This whole affair bore every sign of her light touch, yet she was nowhere in sight. I was shown to a room and met some of the officers on the Count's staff. One of them, Kurt, a youth of noble lineage but no money, showed me around the grounds. The place was a cross between a feudal keep and a small town, with a high wall cutting it off from the city proper. There appeared to be no obvious signs of the Count's plans, outside of the number of armed retainers who lounged about and practiced uninterestedly in the shooting ranges. It all looked too peaceful to be true – yet I had been brought here. That was no accident. I tried a little delicate questioning and Kurt was frank with his answers. Like a lot of the far-country gentry he bore a grudge against the central authorities, although he would of course never have gotten around to doing anything about it on his own. Somehow he had been recruited and was ready to go along with the plans, all of which were very vague to him. I doubt if he had ever seen a corpse. That he wasn't telling me the truth about everything was obvious when I caught him in his first lie.

We had passed some women and bent a knee, and Kurt had volunteered the advice that they were the wives of two of the other officers.

'And you're married too?' I asked.

'No. Never had the time, I guess. Now I suppose it's too late, at least for awhile. When this whole business is over and life is a little more peaceful there'll be plenty of time to settle down.'

'How right,' I agreed. 'What about the Count? Is he married? I've been away so many years that it's hard to keep track of that kind of thing. Wives, children and such.' Without being obvious I was watching him when I asked this, and he gave a little start.

'Well . . . yes, you might say. I mean the Count was married, but there was an accident, he's not married now . . .' His voice tapered away and he drew my attention to something else, happy to leave the topic.

Now if there is one thing that always marks Angelina's trail it is a corpse or two. It took no great amount of inspiration to connect her with the 'accidental' death of the Count's wife. If the death had been natural Kurt would not have been afraid to talk about it. He didn't mention the topic again and I made no attempt to pump him. I had my lead. Angelina may not have been in sight – but her spoor was around me on all sides. It was just a matter of time now. As soon as I was able to, I would shake Kurt and hunt up the bully-boys who had spirited me out of the jail. Buy them a few drinks to assure them that there were no hard feelings about the beating they had given me. Then pump them adroitly about the man who had led them.

Angelina made her move first. One of the coal-burning robots came hissing and clanking around with a message. The Count would like to see me. I slicked my hair, tucked in my shirt and reported for duty.

I was pleased to see that the Count was a steady and

solitary daytime drinker. In addition, there was very little tobacco in his cigarette; the sweet smoke filled the room. All this meant he was due for early dissolution, and I would not be numbered among his mourners. None of this showed in my expression or attitude of course. I was all flashing eye and hell-cracking attention.

'Is it action, sir? Is that why you sent for me?' I asked.

'Sit down, sit down,' he mumbled, waving me towards a chair. 'Relax. Want a cigarette?' He pushed the box towards me and I eyed the thin brown cylinders with distaste.

'Not today, sir. I'm laying off smoking for awhile. Sharpening up the old eye. Keeping the old trigger finger limber and ready for action.'

The Count's mind was occupied elsewhere and I doubt if he heard a word I said. He chewed abstractedly at the inside of his cheek while he looked me up and down. A decision finally struggled up through his half-clotted brain.

'What do you know about the Radebrechen family?' he asked, which is about as exotic a question as I have ever had thrown at me.

'Absolutely nothing,' I answered truthfully. 'Should I?'

'No ... no ...' he answered vaguely, and went back to chewing his cheek. I was getting high just from breathing the air in the room and I wondered how he was feeling.

'Come with me,' he said, pushing over his chair and almost falling on top of it. We plodded through a number of halls deeper into the building, until we came to a door, no different from the ones we had passed, except this one had a guard in front of it – a rough-looking brawny type with his arms casually crossed. Just casual enough to let his fingers hang over his pistol grip. He didn't budge when we came up.

'It's all right,' the Duke of Rdenrundt said, with what I swear was a peevish tone. 'He's with me.'

'Gotta search him anyway,' the guard said. 'Orders.'

More and more interesting. Who issued orders the Count couldn't change – in his own castle? As if I didn't know. And I recognized the guard's voice, he was one of the men who had taken me from my prison cell. He searched me quickly and efficiently, then stepped aside. The Count opened the door and I followed him in, trying not to tread on his heels.

One thing about reality – it is always so much superior to theory. I had every reason to believe that Angelina would be here, yet it was still a healthy shock to see her sitting at the table. A kind of electric charge in my spine tingled right up to the roots of my hair. This was a moment I had waited for for a very long time. It took a positive effort to relax and appear indifferent. At least as indifferent as any healthy young male is in front of an attractive package of femininity.

Of course this girl didn't resemble Angelina very much. Yet I still had no doubt. The face was changed as was the color of the hair. And though the face was a new one it still held the same sweet, angelic quality as the old. Her figure was much the way I remembered it, with perhaps a few slight improvements. Hers was a surface transformation, with no attempt at being as complete as the one I had done to me.

'This is Grav Bent Diebstall,' the Count said, fixing his hot and smoky little eyes on her. 'The man you wanted to see, Engela.' So she was still an angel, though under a different name. That was a bad habit she should watch, only I wasn't going to tell her. A lot of people have been caught by taking an alias too similar to their old one.

'Why thank you, Cassitor,' she said. Cassitor indeed! I'd look unhappy too if I had to go through life with a handle like Cassitor Rdenrundt. 'It was very nice of you to bring Grav Bent here,' she added in the same light and empty voice.

Cassi must have been expecting a warmer welcome because he stood first on one foot and then another and mumbled something which neither of us heard. But Angelina-Engela's welcome stayed at the same temperature, or perhaps dropped a degree or two as she shuffled some papers on the table in front of her. Even through his fog the Count caught on and went out mumbling something else under his breath that I was pretty sure was one of the shorter and more unwholesome words in the local dialect. We were alone.

'Why did you tell those lies about being in the Stellar Guard,' she asked in a quiet voice, apparently still busy at the papers. This was my cue to smile sardonically, and flick some imaginary dust from my sleeve.

'Well I certainly couldn't tell all those nice people what I've really been doing all these years I have been away, could I?' I responded with wide-eyed simplicity.

'What were you doing, Bent?' she asked and there wasn't a trace of any emotion in her voice.

'That's really my business, isn't it,' I told her, matching toneless tone for tone. 'And while we're asking questions, I would like to know who you are, and how come you seem to throw more weight around than the great Count Cassitor?' I'm good at playing

151

this kind of guessing game. But Angy was just as good and dragged the conversation back to her own grounds.

'Since I am in the stronger position here, I think you'll find it wise to answer my questions. Don't be afraid of shocking me. You would be surprised at the things I know about.'

No, Angelica love, I wouldn't be surprised at all. But I couldn't just tell all without a little resistance. 'You're the one behind this revolution idea, aren't you,' I said as a statement, not a question.

'Yes,' she said, laying her cards on the table so she could see mine.

'Well if you must know then,' I said, 'I was smuggling. It is a very interesting occupation if you happen to know what to take where. For a number of years I found it was a most lucrative business. Finally though, a number of governments felt I was giving them unfair competition, since they were the only ones allowed to cheat the public. With the pressure on I returned to my sluggish native land for a period of rest.'

Angel-mine was buying no sealed packages and gave me an exhaustive cross-examination into my smuggling career that showed she had more than a passing knowledge of the field herself. I had of course no trouble answering her questions, since in my day I have turned many a megacredit in this illegal fashion. The only thing I was afraid of was making it too good, so I described a career of a successful but still young and not too professional operator. All the time I was talking I tried to live the role and believe everything I said. This was a crucial time when I must let drop no hints or mannerisms that might bring Slippery Jim diGriz to her mind. I had to be the local punk who had made good and was still on my way up in the universe.

Mind you – our talk was of course all most casual, and carried on in an atmosphere of passing drinks and lighting cigarettes all designed to relax me enough to make a few slips. I did of course, slipping in a lie or two about my successes that she would catch and credit to boyish enthusiasm. When the chit-chat slowed I tried a question of my own.

'Would you mind telling me what a local family named Radebrechen has to do with you?'

'What makes you ask?' she said so calm and coolly.

'Your smiling friend Cassitor Rdenrundt asked me about them before we came here. I told him I knew nothing. What's their connection with you?'

'They want to kill me,' she said.

'That would be a shame – and a waste,' I told her with my best come-hither grin. She ignored it. 'What can I do about it?' I asked, going back to business, since she didn't seem interested in my masculine attractions.

'I want you to be my bodyguard,' she said, and when I smiled and opened my mouth to speak she went on, 'and please spare me any remarks about how it is a body you would like to guard. I get enough of that from Cassitor.'

'All I wanted to say was that I accepted the position,' which was a big lie because I had had some such phrase in mind. It was hard to stay ahead of Angelina and I mustn't relax for an instant I reminded myself again. 'Just tell me more about the people who are out to kill you.'

'It seems that Count Rdenrundt was married,' Angelicious said, toying with her glass in a simple, girlish way. 'His wife committed suicide in a very stupid and compromising manner. Her family – who are of course the Radebrechen – think I killed her, and want to revenge her supposed murder by killing me in turn. Apparently in this lost corner of Freibur the vendetta still has meaning, and this family of rich morons still subscribe to it.'

All at once the picture was getting clearer. Count Rdenrundt – a born opportunist – aided his noble fortunes by marrying the daughter of this family. This must have worked well enough until Angelina came along. Then the extra wife was in the way, and ignorant of this charming local custom of revenge-killing, Angelina had removed a stumbling stone. Something had gone wrong – probably the Count had bungled, from the look of the man – and now the vendetta was on. And my Angel wanted me to interpose my frail flesh between her and the killers. Apparently she was finding this retarded planet more than she had bargained for. Now was the time for me to be bold.

'Was it suicide?' I asked, 'Or did you kill her?'

'Yes, I killed her,' she said. The sparring was over and all our cards were on the table. The decision was up to me.

CHAPTER

-17-

Well what else was there to do? I hadn't come this far, getting myself shot, bashed on the head and well-stomped, just to arrest her. I mean I was going to arrest her, of course, but it was next to impossible in the center of the Count's stronghold. Besides that, I wanted to find out a bit more about the Count's proposed uprising, since this would certainly come within the jurisdiction of the Special Corps. If I was going to reenlist I had better bring along a few prizes to show my good intentions.

Anyway – I wasn't so sure I wanted to reenlist. It was a little hard to forget that scuttling charge they had tried to blow up under me. The whole thing wasn't so simple. There were a lot of things mixed up in this. One fact being that I enjoyed Angelina and most of the time I was with her I forgot about those bodies floating in space. They returned at night all right and chopped at my conscience, but I was always tired and went to sleep quickly before they could get through and bother me.

Life was a bed of roses, and I might as well enjoy it before the blossoms withered. Watching Angelady at work was a distinct pleasure, and if you stood my back to the wall and made me swear, I would be forced to admit that I learned a thing or two from her. Singlehandedly she was organizing a revolution of a peaceful planet – and it stood every chance of succeeding. In my small way I helped. The few times she mentioned a problem to me I had a ready answer and in all the cases she went along with my suggestions. Of course I had never toppled governments before, but there are basic laws in crime as in everything else, and it is just a matter of application. This didn't happen often. Most of the time during those first few weeks I was plain bodyguard, keeping a wary eye out for assassins. This position had a certain ironical angle that appealed to me greatly.

However there was a serpent in our little Eden of Insurrection, and his name was Rdenrundt. I never heard much, but from a word caught here and there I began to see that the Count wasn't really cut out to be a revolutionary. The closer we came to the day the more pallid he became. His little physical vices began to add up, and one day the whole thing came to a head.

Angelegant and the Count were in a business session and I sat in the anteroom outside. I shamelessly eavesdropped whenever I could, and this time I had managed to leave the door open a crack after I had checked her into the room. Careful manipulation with my toe opened it a bit more until I could hear the murmur of their voices. An argument was progressing nicely – there were a lot of them at this time – and I could catch a word here and there. The Count was shouting and it was obvious that he wouldn't give in on some simple and necessary piece of blackmail to advance the cause. Then his tone changed and his voice dropped so I couldn't hear his words, strain as I might. There was a saccharine wheedle and whine in his voice, and Angelina's answer was clear enough. A loud and positive *no*. His bellow brought me to my feet.

'Why not? It's always *no* now and I've had enough of it!'

There was the sound of tearing cloth and something fell to the floor and broke. I was through the door in a single bound. For a brief instant I had a glimpse of a struggling tableau as he pulled at her. Angelina's clothing was torn from one shoulder and his fingers were sunk into her arms like claws. Clubbing my pistol I ran forward. Angelina was a bit faster. She pulled a bottle from the table and banged it into the side of his head with neat efficiency. The Count dropped as if he had been shot. She was pulling up her torn blouse when I came roaring to a halt.

'Put the gun away, Bent – it's all over,' she said in a calm voice. I did, but only after making sure the Count was really out, hoping an extra slam might be needed. But she had done a good job. When I stood up Angelina was already halfway out of the room and I had to run to catch up with her. The only other thing she said was 'Wait here,' when she steamed into her room.

It took no great power of divination to see that there was trouble coming – if it hadn't already arrived. When the Count came to with a busted head he would undoubtedly have some second thoughts about Angelina and revolutions. I thought on these and related subjects while I matched coins with the guards. A few minutes later Angelina called me in.

A long robe covered her arms so the bruises he had made weren't visible. Though outwardly composed there was a telltale glint in her eyes that meant she was doing a slow burn. I spoke what was undoubtedly the uppermost thought in her mind.

'Want me to fix it so the Count joins his noble ancestors in the family crypt?'

She shook her head no. 'He still has his uses. I managed to control my temper – so you had better hold yours.'

'Mine's in great shape. But what makes you think you can still get work or cooperation out of him? He's going to have an awful sore head when he comes to.'

Minor factors like this didn't bother her; she dismissed the thought with a wave of her hand. 'I can still handle him and make him do whatever I want – within limits. The limitations are his own natural abilities, which I didn't realize were so slight when I picked him to head this revolt. I'm afraid his cowardice is slowly destroying any large hopes I might have had for him. He will still have value as a figurehead and we must use him for that. But the power and decisions must be ours.'

I wasn't being slow, just wary. I chewed around her statements from all sides before I answered. 'Just what is this *we* and *ours* business? Where do I fit in?'

Angelilith leaned back in her chair and tossed a lock of her lovely golden hair to one side. Her smile had about a two thousand volt charge and was aimed at me.

'I want you to come in with me on this thing,' she said with a voice rich as warm honey. 'A partnership. We'll keep the Count of Rdenrundt out in front until the plan succeeds. Then eliminate him and go the rest of the way ourselves. Do you agree?'

'Well,' I said. Then with brilliant inspiration, 'Well

'...' again. For the first time in a lifetime of verbal pyrotechnics I found the flow shut off. I paced the room and pulled my scattered wits together.

'I hate to look a gift rocket in the tubes,' I told her, 'nevertheless – why *me*? A simple but hard working bodyguard, who will guard your person, labor for the cause and look forward to the restoration of his stolen lands and title. How come the big jump from office boy to board chairman?'

'You know better than to ask that,' she said and smiled, and the temperature of the room rose ten degrees. 'I think you can handle this job as well as I can, and enjoy doing it. Working together, you and I will make this the cleanest revolt that ever took over a planet. What do you say?'

I was pacing behind her as she talked. She stood up and took me by the arm, stilling my restless walking. I could feel the warmth of her fingers burning through my thin shirt. Her face was in front of me, smiling, and her voice pitched so low that I barely heard it.

'It would be something, wouldn't it. You and I ... together.'

Wouldn't it! There are occasions when words can't say it all and your body speaks for you. This was a time like that. Without physical deliberation my arms were around her, pulling her to me, my mouth pushing down on hers.

For the briefest of instants she was the same, her arms tight on my shoulders, her lips alive. Just for a sliver of time so brief that afterwards I couldn't be sure that I hadn't imagined it. Then the warmth was suddenly drained away and everything was wrong.

She didn't fight me or attempt to push back. But her lips were lifeless under mine and her eyes open, looking at me with a sterile emptiness. She did nothing until I had dropped my arms and stepped away, then she seated herself stiffly in the chair again.

'What's wrong?' I asked not trusting myself to say more.

'A pretty face – is that all you think of?' she asked, and the words seemed pulled from her in sobs. Expressing real emotions didn't come easily with her. 'Are you men all alike – all the same—?'

'Nonsense!' I shouted, angered in spite of myself. 'You wanted me to kiss you – don't deny it! What changed your mind?'

'Would you want to kiss *her*?' Angelina screamed, torn by emotions I couldn't understand. She pulled at a thin chain around her neck. It snapped and she half threw it at me. There was a tiny locket on the chain, still warm from her body. It had an image-enlarger in it, and when held at the right angle the picture inside could be seen clearly. I had the chance for only a single glimpse at the girl in the photograph, then Angelina changed her mind and pulled it away, pushing me towards the door at the same time. It slammed behind me and I heard the heavy safety bolts thud home.

Ignoring the guard's raised eyebrows I stamped down the hall to my own room. My emotions had triumphed nicely over my powers of reason, and apparently Angelina's had too – for just an instant. Yet I couldn't understand her cold withdrawal or the significance of the picture. Why did she wear it?

I had only had a single glimpse of the contents but that was enough. It was the photo of a young girl, a sister perhaps? A tragic thing, one of those horrible proofs of the law of chance that an almost infinite number of combinations are possible. This girl was cursed with ugliness, that is the only way to describe it. It was no single factor of a bent back, adenoidal jaw or protruding nose. Instead it was the damning combination of traits that combined to form a single, repellent whole. I didn't like it. But what did it matter. . . .

I sat down suddenly with the clear realization that I was being incredibly stupid. Angelina had given me a simple brief glimpse into the dark motivations that had made her, shaped her life.

Of course. The girl in the picture was Angelina herself.

With this realization so many other things became clear. Many times when looking at her I had wondered why that deadly mind should be housed in such an attractive package. The answer was clearly that I wasn't looking at the original package that had shaped the mind. To be a man and to be ugly is bad enough. What must it feel like to be a woman? How do you live when mirrors are your enemies and people turn away rather than look at you? How do you bear life when at the same time you are blessed – or cursed – with a keen and intelligent mind that sees and is aware of everything, makes the inescapable conclusions and misses not the slightest hint of repulsion?

Some girls might commit suicide, but not Angelina. I could guess what she had done. Hating herself, loathing and detesting her world and the people on it, she would have had no compunction about committing a crime to gain the money she wanted. Money for an operation to correct one of those imperfections. Then more money for more operations. Then someone who dared to stop her in this task, and the ease and perhaps pleasure with which she killed him. The slow upward climb through crime and murder – to beauty.

And during the climb the wonderful brain that had been housed in the illformed flesh had been warped and changed.

Poor Angelina. I could be sorry for her without forgetting the ones she had killed. Poor, tragic, alone girl who in winning half the battle had lost the other half. Purchased skill had shaped the body into a lovely – truthfully an angelic – form. Yet in succeeding, the strength of the mind that had accomplished all this had been deformed until it had been made as ugly as the body had been in the beginning.

Yet if you could change a body – couldn't you change a mind? Could something be done for her?

The very pressure and magnitude of my thoughts drove me out of the small room and into the air. It was nearing midnight and the guards would be stationed below and all the doors locked. Rather than face the explanations and simple mechanical difficulties, I climbed upwards instead. There would be no one in the roofgardens and walkways this time of night; I could be alone.

Freibur has no moon, but it was a clear night and the stars cast enough light to see by. The roof guard saluted when I went by, and I could see the red spark of a cigarette in his hand. I should have said something about it, but my mind was too occupied. Passing on I turned a corner and stood leaning on the parapet, looking out unseeingly at the black bulk of the mountains.

Something kept gnawing for attention and after a few minutes I recognized what it was. The guard. He was there for a purpose, and smoking on duty wasn't considered the best behavior for a sentry. Perhaps I was being finicky, but it is a failing of mine. Take care of all the small factors and the big ones take care of themselves. In any case, simply thinking about it was bothering me, so I might as well go around and say a word to him.

He wasn't at his usual post, which was optimistic; at least he was making the rounds and keeping an eye on things. I started to walk back when I noticed the broken flowers hanging from the edge of the garden. This was most unusual because the roofgardens were the Count's special pleasure and were practically manicured daily. Then I saw the dark patch in among the flowers and had the first intimation that something was very, very wrong.

It was the guard, and he was either dead or deeply unconscious. I didn't bother to find out which. There was only one reason I could think of for someone to be here at night like this. Angelina. Her room was on the top floor, almost below this spot. Silently I ran to the decorative railing and looked over. Five meters below was the white patch of the balcony outside her window. Something black and formless was crouched there.

My gun was in my room. For one of the few times in my life I had been so disturbed that my normal precautions were forgotten. My concern over Angelina was going to cost her her life.

All of this I realized in a fraction of a second as my fingers ran along the balustrade. A shiny blob was fixed there, anchoring a strand so thin that it was invisible, yet I knew was as strong as a cable. The assassin had lowered himself with a web-spinner, a tiny device that spun a thin strand like a spider. Only the strand's substance was formed on a single long-chain molecule that could support a man's weight. It would slice my hands like the sharpest blade if I tried to slide down it.

There was only one way I could reach that balcony, a tiny square above the two kilometer drop into the valley below. I made the decision even as I was leaping up onto the rail. It had a wide flat top and I sat for an instant to catch my balance. Below me the window swung open noiselessly and I dropped, my heels extended, aiming for the man below.

I turned in the air and instead of hitting him squarely I caromed off his shoulder and we both sprawled onto the balcony. It shivered under the impact, but the ancient stone held. The fall had half-stunned me, and with pain-blurred reasoning I hoped that his shoulder felt as bad as my leg. For a few moments I could do nothing but gasp for breath and try to scramble towards him. A long, thin-bladed knife had been knocked from his hand by the impact and I could see it glittering where he reached for it. His fingers clutched it just as I attacked. He grunted and made a vicious stab at me that brushed my sleeve. Before he could draw back I had his knife wrist in my hand and clamped on.

It was a silent, nightmare battle. Both of us were half-dazed from my drop, yet we knew it was life we were battling for. I couldn't stand because of my bruised leg and he was instantly on top of me, heavier and stronger. He couldn't use the arm I had landed on, but it took all the strength of both my arms to hold away the menacing blade. There was no sound other than our hoarse panting.

This assassin was going to win as weight and remorseless strength brought the knife down. Sweat almost blinded me, but I could still see well enough to notice the twisted way his other arm hung. I had broken a bone when I hit – yet he had never made a sound.

There is no such thing as fair fighting when you are struggling for your life. I squirmed my leg out from under him and managed to bend it enough to dig the knee into his broken arm. His whole body shuddered. I did it again. Harder. He twisted, trying to pull away from the pain. I heaved sideways, throwing him off balance. His elbow bent as he tried to save himself from falling and I put all my strength in both hands turning that sinewy wrist and driving the hand backwards.

It almost worked, but he was still stronger than I was and the point of the blade merely scratched his chest. Even as I was fighting to turn the hand again he shuddered and died.

A ruse would not have tricked me – but this was no ruse. I felt every muscle in his body tighten rock-hard in a spasm as he fell sideways. My grip on his wrist didn't lessen until the light came on in the room behind me. Only then did I see the ugly yellow stain halfway up the blade of the knife. A quick-acting nerve poison, silent and deadly. There, on the sleeve of my shirt, was a thin yellow mark where the blade had brushed me. I knew these poisons didn't need a puncture, they could work just as well on the naked skin.

With infinite caution, struggling against the fatigue that wanted my hands to shake, I peeled my shirt slowly off. Only when it had been hurled on top of the corpse did I let myself drop backwards, gasping for air.

My leg could work now, though it hurt hideously. It must have been bruised but not broken since it supported my weight. Turning, I stumbled to the high window and threw it open. Light streamed out on the body behind me. Angelina was sitting up in bed, her face smooth and her hands folded on the covers in front of her. Only her eyes showing any awareness of what had happened.

'Dead,' I said with a dry throat, and spat to clear it. 'Killed by his own poison.' I stumped into the room, testing my leg.

'I was sleeping, I didn't hear him open the window,' she said. 'Thank you.'

Actress, liar, cheat, murderess. She had played a hundred roles in countless voices. Yet when she said those final words there was a ring of unforged feeling to them. This murder attempt had come too soon after the earlier traumatic scene. Her defenses were still down, her real emotions showing.

Her hair hung to her shoulders, brushing the single ribbons on her nightgown which was made of some thin and soft fabric; intimate. This sight, on top of the events of the evening, removed any reserve I might have had. I was kneeling by the bed, holding her shoulders and staring deep into her eyes, trying to reach what lay behind them. The locket with the broken chain lay on the bedside table. I grabbed it in my fist.

'Don't you realize this girl doesn't exist except in your own memory,' I said, and Angelina didn't move. 'It's past like everything else. You were a baby – now you're a woman. You were a little girl – now you're a woman. You may have been this girl – but you are not any more!'

With a convulsive movement I turned and hurled the thing out of the window into the darkness.

'You're none of those things of the past, Angelina!' I

said with an intensity louder than a shout. 'You are yourself … just yourself!'

I kissed her then and there was no trace of the pushing away or rejection there had been before. As I needed her, she needed me.

CHAPTER
-18-

Dawn was just touching the sky when I brought the assassin's body in to the Count. I was deprived of the pleasure of waking him since the sergeant of the guard had already done this when the roof sentry had been discovered. The guard was dead too, from a tiny puncture of the same poison-tipped blade. The guardsmen and the Count were all gathered around the body on the floor of the Count's sitting room and chattering away about this mystery, the inexplicable death of the sentry. They didn't see me until I dropped my corpse down by the other one, and they all jumped back.

'Here's the killer,' I told them, not without a certain amount of pride. Count Cassitor must have recognized the thug because he gave a shuddering start and popped his eyes. No doubt an ex-relative, brother-in-law or something. I imagined he hadn't believed that the Radebrechen family would really go through with their threats of revenge.

A certain uneasiness about the guard sergeant gave me my first cue that I was imagining wrong. The sergeant glanced back and forth from the corpse to the Count and I wondered what thoughts were going through his shaven and thick-skulled military head.

There were wheels within wheels here and I would like to have known what was going on. I made a mental note to have a buddy-to-buddy talk with sarge at the first opportunity. The Count chewed his cheek and cracked his knuckles over the bodies, and finally ordered them dragged out.

'Stay here, Bent,' he said as I started to leave with the others. I dropped into a chair while he locked the rest out. Then he made a rush for the bar and choked down about a waterglass full of the local spirits. Only when he was working on his second glass did he remember to offer me some of this potable aqua regia. I wasn't saying no, and while I sipped at it I wondered what he was so upset about.

First the Count checked the locks on all the doors and sealed the single window. His ring key unlocked the bottom drawer of his desk and he took out a small electronic device with controls and an extendible aerial on top.

'Well look at that!' I said when he pulled out the aerial. He didn't answer me, just shot a long look at me from under his eyebrows, and went back to adjusting the thing. Only when it was turned on and the green light glowed on the top did he relax a bit.

'You know what this is?' he asked, pointing at the gadget.

'Of course,' I said. 'But not from seeing them on Freibur. They aren't that common.'

'They aren't common at all,' he mumbled, staring at the green light which glowed steadily. 'As far as I know this is the only one on the planet – so I wish you wouldn't mention it to anybody. *Anybody*,' he repeated with emphasis.

'Not my business,' I told him with disarming lack of interest. 'I think a man's entitled to his privacy.'

I liked privacy myself and had used snooper-detectors like this one plenty of times. They could sense electronic or radiation snoopers and gave instant warning. There were ways of fooling them, but it wasn't easy to do. As long as no one knew about the thing the Count could be sure he wasn't being eavesdropped on. But who would want to do that? He was in the middle of his own building – and even he must know that snooper devices couldn't be worked from a distance. There was distinct smell of rat in the air, and I was beginning to get an idea of what was going on. The Count didn't leave me any doubt as to who the rat was.

'You're not a stupid man, Grav Diebstall,' he said, which means he thought I was a lot stupider than he was. 'You've been offplanet and seen other worlds. You know how backward and suppressed we are here, or you wouldn't have joined with me to help throw off the yoke around our planet's neck. No sacrifice is too great if it will bring closer this day of liberation.' For some reason he was sweating now and had resumed his unpleasant habit of cracking the knuckles. The side of his head – where Angela had landed the bottle – was covered with plastiskin and dry of sweat. I hoped it hurt.

'This foreign woman you have been guarding—' the Count said, turning sideways but still watching me from the corners of his eyes. 'She had been of some help in organizing things, but is now putting us in an embarrassing position. There has been one attempt on her life and there will probably be others. The Radebrechen are an old and loyal family – her presence is a continued insult to them.' Then he pulled at his drink and delivered the punch line.

'I think that *you* can do the job she is doing. Just as well, and perhaps better. How would you like that?'

Without a doubt I was just brimming over with talent – or there was a shortage of revolutionaries on this planet. This was the second time within twelve hours that I had been offered a partnership in the new order. One thing I was sure of though – Angelovely's offer had been sincere. Cassi Duke of Rdenrunt's proposition had a distinctly bad odor to it. I played along to see what he was leading up to.

'I am honored, noble Count,' I oozed. 'But what will happen to the foreign woman? I don't imagine she will think much of the idea.'

'What she thinks is not important,' he snarled and touched his fingers lightly to the side of his head. He swallowed and got his temper back under control. 'We cannot be cruel to her,' he said with one of the most insincere smiles I have ever seen on a human being's face. 'We'll just hold her in custody. She has some guards who I imagine will be loyal, but my men will take care of them. You will be with her and arrest her at the proper time. Just turn her over to the jailers who will keep her safe. Safe for herself, and out of sight where she can cause no more trouble for us.'

'It's a good plan,' I agreed with winning insincerity. 'I don't enjoy the thought of putting this poor woman in jail, but if it is necessary to the cause it must be done. The ends justify the means.'

'You're right. I only wish I was able to state it so clearly. You have a remarkable ability to turn a phrase, Bent. I'm going to write that down so I can remember it. The ends justify ...'

He scratched away industriously on a note plate. What a knowledge of history he had – just the man to plan a revolution! I searched my memory for a few more old saws to supply him with, until my brain was flooded with a sudden anger. I jumped to my feet.

'If we are going to do this we should not waste any time, Count Rdenrundt,' I said. 'I suggest 1800 hours tonight for the action. That will give you enough time to arrange for the capture of her guards. I will be in her rooms and will arrest her as soon as I have a message from you that the first move has succeeded.'

'You're correct. A man of action as always, Bent. It will be as you say.' We shook hands then and it took all the will power I possessed to stop from crushing to a pulp his limp, moist, serpentine paw. I went straight to Angelina.

'Can we be overheard here?' I asked her.

'No, the room is completely shielded.'

'Your former boy-friend, Count Cassi, has a snooper-detector. He may have other equipment for listening to what goes on here.'

This thought didn't bother Angelic in the slightest. She sat by the mirror, brushing her hair. The scene was lovely but distracting. There were strong winds blowing through the revolution that threatened to knock everything down.

'I know about the detector,' she said calmly, brushing. 'I arranged for him to get it – without his knowledge of course – and made sure it was useless on the best frequencies. I keep a close watch on his affairs that way.'

'Were you listening in a few minutes ago when he was making arrangements with me to kill your guards and throw you into the dungeons downstairs?'

'No, I wasn't listening,' she said with that amazing self-possession and calm that marked all her actions. She smiled in the mirror at me. 'I was busy just remembering last night.'

Women! They insist on mixing everything up together. Perhaps they operate better that way, but it is very hard on those of us who find that keeping emotion and logic separate produces sounder thinking. I had to make her understand the seriousness of this situation.

'Well, if that little bit of news doesn't interest you,' I said as calmly as I could, 'perhaps this does. The rough Radebrechens didn't send that killer last night – the Count did.'

Success at last. Angelina actually stopped combing her hair and her eyes widened a bit at the import of what I said. She didn't ask any stupid questions, but waited for me to finish.

'I think you have underestimated the desperation of that rat upstairs. When you dropped him with that bottle yesterday, you pushed him just as far as he could be pushed. He must have had his plans already made and you made his mind up for him. The sergeant of the guard recognized the assassin and connected him with the Count. That also explains how the killer got access to the roof and knew just where to find you. It's also the best explanation I can imagine for the suddenness of this attack. There's too much coincidence here with the thing happening right after your battle with Cassitor the Cantankerous.'

Angelina had gone back to combing her hair while I talked, fluffing up the curls. She made no response. Her apparent lack of interest was beginning to try my nerves.

'Well – what are you going to do about it?' I asked, with more than a little note of peevishness in my voice.

'Don't you think it's more important to ask what *you* are going to do about it?' She delivered this line very lightly, but there was a lot behind it. I saw she was watching me in the mirror, so I turned and went over to the window, looking out over the fatal balcony at the snow-summitted mountain peaks beyond. What was I going to do about it? Of course that was the question here – much bigger than she realized.

What was I going to do about the whole thing? Everyone was offering me half-interests in a revolution I hadn't the slightest interest in. Or did I? What *was* I doing here? Had I come to arrest Angelina for the Special Corps? That assignment seemed to have been forgotten a while back. A decision had to be reached soon. My body disguise was good – but not that good. It wasn't intended to stand up to long inspection. Only the fact that Angelina was undoubtedly sure that she had killed me had prevented her from recognizing my real identity so far. I had certainly recognized her easily enough, facial changes and all.

Just at this point the bottom dropped out of everything. There is a little process called selective forgetting whereby we suppress and distort memories we find distasteful. My disguise hadn't been meant to stand inspection this long. Originally I had been sure she would have penetrated it by now. With this realization came the memory of what I had said the night before. A wickedly revealing statement that I had pushed back and forgotten until now.

You're none of these things out of the past. I had shouted. *None of these things ... Angelina.* I had bellowed this and there had been no protest from her.

Except that she no longer used the name Angelina, she used the alias Engela here.

When I turned to face her my guilty thoughts must have been scrawled all over my face, but she only gave me that enigmatic smile and said nothing. At least she had stopped combing her hair.

'You know I'm not Grav Bent Diebstall,' I said with an effort. 'How long have you known?'

'For quite a while; since soon after you came here, in fact.'

'Do you know who I am—?'

'I have no idea what your real name is, if that's what you mean. But I do remember how angry I was when you tricked me out of the battleship, after all my work. And I recall the intense satisfaction with which I shot you in Freiburbad. Can you tell me your name now?'

'Jim,' I said through the haze I was rooted in. 'James diGriz, known as Slippery Jim to the trade.'

'How nice. My name *is* really Angela. I think it was done as a horrid joke by my father, which is one of the reasons I enjoyed seeing him die.'

'Why haven't you killed me?' I asked, having a fairly good idea of how father had passed on.

'Why should I, darling?' she asked, and her light, empty tone was gone. 'We've both made mistakes in the past and it has taken us a dreadfully long time to find out that we are just alike. I might as well ask you why you haven't arrested me – that's what you started out to do isn't it?'

'It was – but ...'

'But, what? You must have come here with that idea in mind, but you were fighting an awful battle with yourself. That's why I hid the fact that I knew who you really were. You were growing up, getting over whatever idiotic notions ever involved you with the police in the first place. I had no idea how the whole thing would come out, though I did hope. You see I didn't want to kill you, not unless I had to. I knew you loved me, that was obvious from the beginning. It was different from the feeble animal passion of all those male brutes who have told me that they love me. They loved a malleable case of flesh. You love me for everything that I am, because we are both the same.'

'We are not the same,' I insisted, but there was no conviction in my voice. She only smiled. 'You kill – and enjoy killing – that's our basic difference. Don't you see that?'

'Nonsense!' She dismissed the idea with an airy wave. 'You killed last night – rather a good job too – and I didn't notice any reluctance on your part. In fact, wasn't there a certain amount of enthusiasm?'

I don't know why, but I felt as if a noose was tightening around my neck. Everything she said was wrong – but I couldn't see where it was wrong. Where was the way out, the solution that would solve everything?

'Let's leave Freibur,' I said at last. 'Get away from this monstrous and unnecessary rebellion. There will be deaths and killing and no need for them.'

'We'll go – if we go someplace where we can do just as well,' Angela said, and there was a hardness back in her voice. 'That's not the major point though. There's something you are going to have to settle in your own mind before you will be happy. This stupid importance you attach to death. Don't you realize how completely trivial it is? Two hundred years from now you, I and every person now living in the galaxy will be dead. What does it matter if a few of them are helped along and reach their destination a bit quicker? They'd do the same to you if they had the chance.'

'You're wrong,' I insisted, knowing that there is more to living and dying than just this pessimistic philosophy, but unable in this moment of stress to clarify and speak my ideas. Angela was a powerful drug and my tiny remaining shard of compassionate reserve didn't stand a chance, washed under by the flood of stronger emotions. I pulled her to me, kissing her, knowing that this solved most of the problems although it made the final solution that much more difficult.

A thin and irritating buzz scratched at my ears, and Angela heard it too. Separating was difficult for both of us. I sat and watched unseeingly while she went to the vidiphone. She blanked the video circuits and snapped a query into it. I couldn't hear the answer because she had the speaker off and listened through the earpiece. Once or twice she said *yes* and looked up suddenly at me. There was no indication of whom she was talking to, and I hadn't the slightest interest. There were problems enough around.

After hanging up she just stood quietly for a moment and I waited for her to speak. Instead she walked to her dressing table and opened the drawer. There were a lot of things that could have been concealed there, but she took out the one thing I was least suspecting.

A gun. Big barreled and deadly, pointing at me.

'Why did you do it, Jim?' she asked, tears in the corners of her eyes. 'Why did you want to do it?'

She didn't even hear my baffled answer. Her thoughts were on herself – though the recoilless never wavered from a point aimed midway in my skull. With alarming suddenness she straightened up and angrily brushed at her eyes.

'You didn't do anything,' she said with the old hard chill on her words. 'I did it myself because I let myself believe that one man could be any different from the others. You have taught me a valuable lesson, and out of gratitude I will kill you quickly, instead of in the way I would much prefer.'

'What the hell are you talking about,' I roared, completely baffled.

'Don't play the innocent to the very end,' she said, as she reached carefully behind her and drew a small heavy bag from under the bed. 'That was the radar post. I installed the equipment myself and have the operators bribed to give me first notice. A ring of ships – as you well know – has dropped from space and surrounded this area. Your job was to keep me occupied so I wouldn't notice this. The plan came perilously close to succeeding.' She put a coat over her arm and backed across the room.

'If I told you I was innocent – gave you my most sincere word of honor – would you believe me?' I asked. 'I have nothing to do with this and know nothing about it.'

'Hooray for the Boy Space Scout,' Angela said with bitter mockery. 'Why don't you admit the truth, since you will be dead in twenty seconds no matter what you say.'

'I've told you the truth.' I wondered if I could reach her before she fired, but knew it was impossible.

'Good-by, James diGriz. It was nice knowing you – for a while. Let me leave you with a last pleasant thought. All this was in vain. There is a door and an exit behind me that no one knows about. Before your police get here I shall be safely gone. And if the thought tortures you a bit, I intend to go on killing and killing and killing and you will never be able to stop me.'

My Angela raised the gun for a surer aim as she touched a switch in the molding. A panel rolled back revealing a square of blackness in the wall.

'Spare me the histrionics, Jim,' she said disgustedly, her eyes looking into mine over the sight of the gun. Her finger tightened. 'I wouldn't expect that kind of juvenile trick from you, staring over my shoulder and widening your eyes as if there was someone behind me. I'm not going to turn and look. You're not getting out of this one alive.'

'Famous last words,' I said as I jumped sideways. The gun boomed but the bullet plowed into the ceiling. Inskipp stood behind her, twisting the gun into the air, pulling it out of her hand. Angela just stared at me in horror and made no move to resist. There were handcuffs locked on her tiny wrists and she still didn't struggle or cry out. I jumped forward, shouting her name.

There were two burly types in Patrol uniforms behind Inskipp, and they took her. Before I could reach the door he stepped through and closed it behind him. I stumbled to a halt before it, as unable to fight as Angela had been a minute ago.

CHAPTER
— 19 —

'Have a drink,' Inskipp said, dropping into Angela's chair and pulling out a hip flask. 'Ersatz terran brandy, not this local brand of plastic solvent.' He offered me a cupful.

'Drop dead, you ...' I followed with some of the choicer selections from my interstellar vocabulary, and tried to knock the cup out of his hand. He fooled me by raising it and drinking it himself, not in the least annoyed.

'Is that any kind of language to use on your superior officer in the Special Corps?' He asked and refilled the cup. 'It's a good thing we're a relaxed organization without too many rules. Still – there are limits.' He held out the cup again and this time I grabbed it and drained it.

'Why did you do it?' I asked, still wracked by conflicting emotions.

'Because you didn't, that's why. The operation is over, you are a success. Before you were merely on probation, but now you are a full agent.'

He grubbed in one pocket and pulled out a little gold star made of paper. After licking it carefully solemnly he reached out and stuck it to the front of my shirt.

'I hereby appoint you a full Agent of the Special Corps,' he intoned, 'by authority of the power vested in me.'

Cursing, I reached to pick the damn thing off – and laughed instead. It was absurd. It was also a fine commentary on the honors that went with the job.

'I thought I was no longer a member of the crew,' I told him.

'I never received your resignation,' Inskipp said. 'Not that it would have meant anything. You can't resign from the Corps.'

'Yeah – but I got your message when you gave me a discharge. Or did you forget that I stole a ship and you set off the scuttling charge by remote to blow me up? As you see I managed to pull the fuse just before it let go.'

'Nothing of the sort, my boy,' he said, settling back to sip his second drink. 'You were so insistent about looking for the fair Angelina that I thought you might want to borrow a ship before we had a chance to assign you one. The one you took had the fuse rigged as it always is on these occasions. The fuse – not the charge – is set to explode five seconds *after* it is removed. I find this gives a certain independence of mind to prospective agents who regret their manner of departure.'

'You mean – the whole thing was a frame-up?' I gurgled.

'You might say that. I prefer the term "graduating-exercise". This is the time when we find out if our crooked novices really will devote the rest of their lives to the pursuit of law and order. When they find out, too. We don't want there to be any regrets in later years. You found out, didn't you Jim?'

'I found out something ... I'm not quite sure what yet,' I said, still not able to talk about the one thing closest to me.

'It was a fine operation. I must say you showed a lot of imagination in the way you carried it out.' Then he frowned. 'But that business with the bank, I can't say I approve of it. The Corps has all the funds you will need ...'

'Same money,' I snapped. 'Where does the Corps get it? From planetary governments. And where do they get it from? Taxes of course. So I take it directly from the bank. The insurance company pays the bank for the loss, then declares a smaller income that year, pays less taxes to the government – and the result is exactly the same as your way!'

Inskipp was well acquainted with this brand of logic so didn't even bother to answer. I still didn't want to talk about Angela.

'How did you find me?' I asked. 'There was no bug on the ship.'

'Simple child of nature that you are,' Inskipp said, raising his hands in feigned horror. 'Do you really think that any of our ships *aren't* bugged? And the job done so well it cannot be detected if you don't know where to look. For your information the apparently solid outer door of the spacelock contains quite a complex transmitter, strong enough for us to detect at quite a distance.'

'Then why didn't I hear it?'

'For the simple reason that it wasn't broadcasting. I should add that the door also contains a receiver. The device only transmits when it receives the proper signal. We gave you time to reach your destination and then followed you. We lost you for a while in Freiburbad, but picked up your trail again in the hospital, right after you played musical chairs with the corpses. We lent you a hand there, the hospital was justifiably annoyed but we managed to keep them quiet. After that it was just a matter of keeping an eye on doctors and surgical equipment since your next move was obvious. I hope you'll be pleased to know that you are carrying a very compact transmitter in your sternum.'

I looked at my chest but of course saw nothing.

'It was too good an opportunity to miss,' Inskipp went on. There was no stopping the man. 'One night when you were under sedation the good doctor found the alcohol we had seen fit to include in one of your supply packages. He of couse took advantage of this shipping error and a Corps surgeon made a little operation of his own.'

'Then you have been following me and watching ever since?'

'That's right. But this was your case, just as much as it would have been if you knew we were there.'

'Then why did you move in for the kill like this?' I snapped. 'I didn't blow the whistle for the marines.'

This was the big question for the hour and the only one that mattered to me. Inskipp took his time about answering.

'It's like this,' he drawled, and took a sip of his drink. 'I like a new man to have enough rope. But not so much that he will hang himself. You were here for what might be called a goodly long time, and I wasn't receiving any reports about revolutions or arrests you had made.'

What could I say?

His voice was quieter, more sympathetic. 'Would *you* have arrested her if we hadn't moved in?' That was the question.

'I don't know,' was all I could say.

'Well I damn well knew what I was going to do,' he said with the old venom. 'So I did it. The plot is well nipped before it could bud and our multiple murderess is offplanet by now.'

'Let her go!' I shouted as I grabbed him by the front of the jacket and swung him free of the ground and shook him. 'Let her go I tell you!'

'Would you turn her loose again – the way she is?' was all he answered.

Would I? I suppose I wouldn't. I dropped him while I was thinking about it and he straightened out the wrinkles in the front of his suit.

'This has been a rough assigment for you,' he said as he started to put the flask away. 'At times there can be a very thin line between right and wrong. If you are emotionally involved the line is almost impossible to see.'

'What will happen to her?' I asked.

He hesitated before he answered. 'The truth – for a change,' I told him.

'All right, the truth. No promises – but the psych boys might be able to do something with her. If they can find the cause of the basic aberration. But that can be impossible to find at times.'

'Not in this case – I can tell them.'

He looked surprised at that, giving me some small satisfaction.

'In that case there might be a chance. I'll give positive orders that everything is to be tried before they even consider anything like personality removal. If that is done she is just another body, of which there are plenty in the galaxy. Sentenced to death she's just another corpse – of which there is an equal multitude.'

I grabbed the flask away from him before it reached his pocket, and opened it. 'I know you, Inskipp,' I said as I poured. 'You're a born recruiting sergeant. When you lick them – make them join.'

'What else,' he said. 'She'd make a great agent.'

'We'd make a great team,' I told him and we raised our cups.

'*Here's to crime.*'